GOSCINNY AND UDERZO

PRESENT

An Asterix Adventure

OBELIX
& CO.

Written by RENÉ GOSCINNY *and Illustrated by* ALBERT UDERZO

Translated by Anthea Bell *and* Derek Hockridge

Orion

Asterix titles available now

ORION CHILDREN'S BOOKS

This revised edition first published in 2004 by Orion Books Ltd
This edition published in 2016 by Hodder and Stoughton

1 3 5 7 9 10 8 6 4 2

ASTERIX®-OBELIX®-DOGMATIX®
© 1976 GOSCINNY/UDERZO
Revised edition and English translation © 2004 Hachette Livre
Original title: *Obélix et Compagnie*
Exclusive licensee: Hachette Children's Group
Translators: Anthea Bell and Derek Hockridge
Typography: Bryony Newhouse

A CIP record for this book is available from the British Library

ISBN 978-0-7528-6651-2 (cased)
ISBN 978-0-7528-6652-9 (paperback)
ISBN 978-1-4440-1330-6 (ebook)

Printed in China

Orion Children's Books
An imprint of Hachette Children's Group, part of Hodder and Stoughton
Carmelite House, 50 Victoria Embankment
London EC4Y 0DZ
An Hachette UK Company

www.hachette.co.uk
www.asterix.com
www.hachettechildrens.co.uk

Asterix and Obelix
@lartdasterix

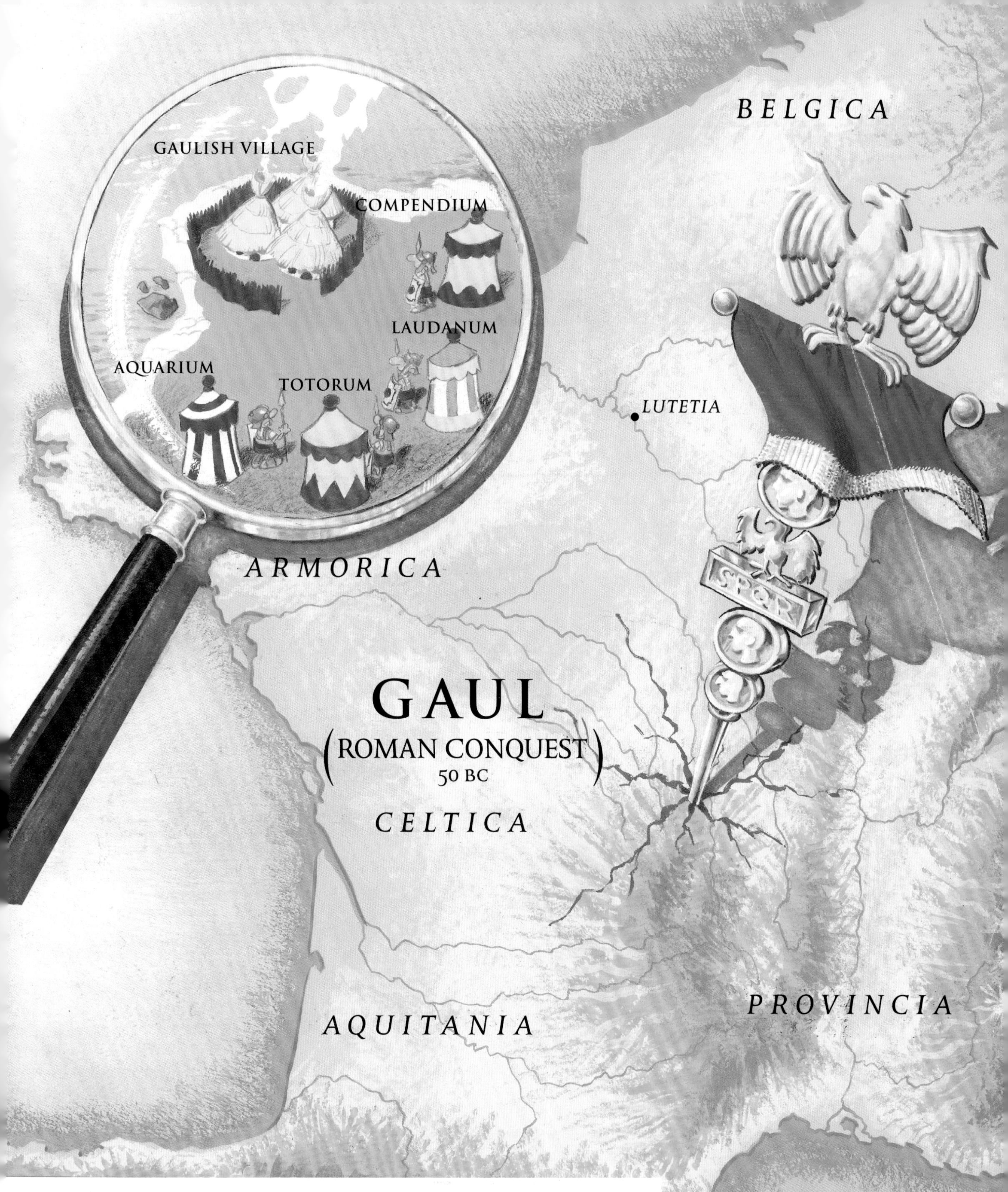
BELGICA
GAULISH VILLAGE
COMPENDIUM
LAUDANUM
AQUARIUM
TOTORUM
LUTETIA
SPQR
ARMORICA
GAUL
(ROMAN CONQUEST)
50 BC
CELTICA
PROVINCIA
AQUITANIA

THE YEAR IS 50 BC. GAUL IS ENTIRELY OCCUPIED BY THE ROMANS. WELL, NOT ENTIRELY ... ONE SMALL VILLAGE OF INDOMITABLE GAULS STILL HOLDS OUT AGAINST THE INVADERS. AND LIFE IS NOT EASY FOR THE ROMAN LEGIONARIES WHO GARRISON THE FORTIFIED CAMPS OF TOTORUM, AQUARIUM, LAUDANUM AND COMPENDIUM ...

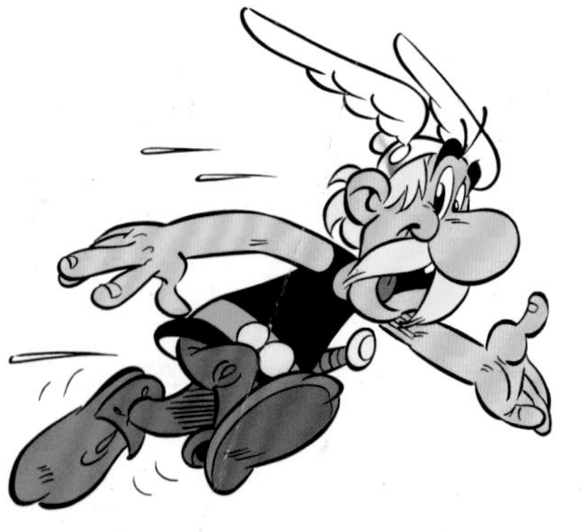

ASTERIX, THE HERO OF THESE ADVENTURES. A SHREWD, CUNNING LITTLE WARRIOR, ALL PERILOUS MISSIONS ARE IMMEDIATELY ENTRUSTED TO HIM. ASTERIX GETS HIS SUPERHUMAN STRENGTH FROM THE MAGIC POTION BREWED BY THE DRUID GETAFIX . . .

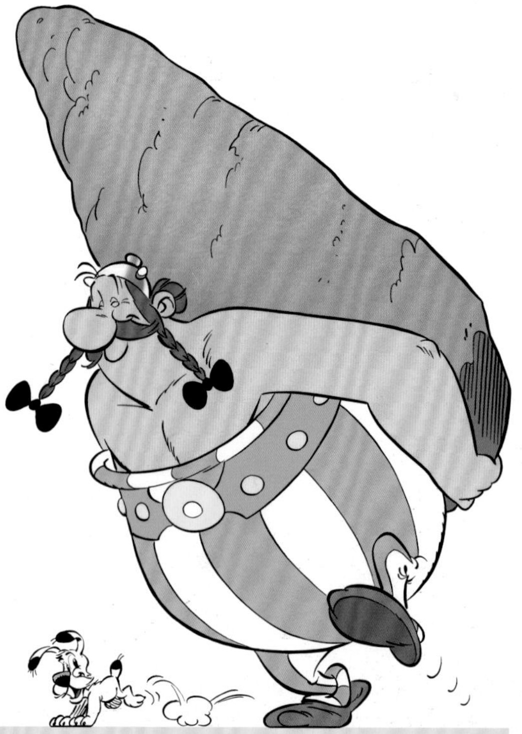

OBELIX, ASTERIX'S INSEPARABLE FRIEND. A MENHIR DELIVERY MAN BY TRADE, ADDICTED TO WILD BOAR. OBELIX IS ALWAYS READY TO DROP EVERYTHING AND GO OFF ON A NEW ADVENTURE WITH ASTERIX – SO LONG AS THERE'S WILD BOAR TO EAT, AND PLENTY OF FIGHTING. HIS CONSTANT COMPANION IS DOGMATIX, THE ONLY KNOWN CANINE ECOLOGIST, WHO HOWLS WITH DESPAIR WHEN A TREE IS CUT DOWN.

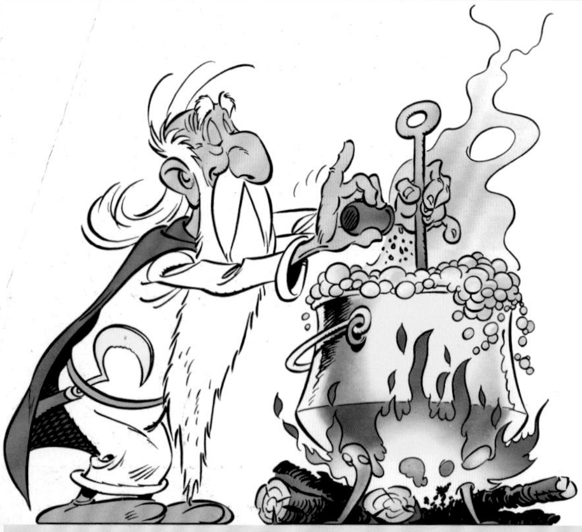

GETAFIX, THE VENERABLE VILLAGE DRUID, GATHERS MISTLETOE AND BREWS MAGIC POTIONS. HIS SPECIALITY IS THE POTION WHICH GIVES THE DRINKER SUPERHUMAN STRENGTH. BUT GETAFIX ALSO HAS OTHER RECIPES UP HIS SLEEVE . . .

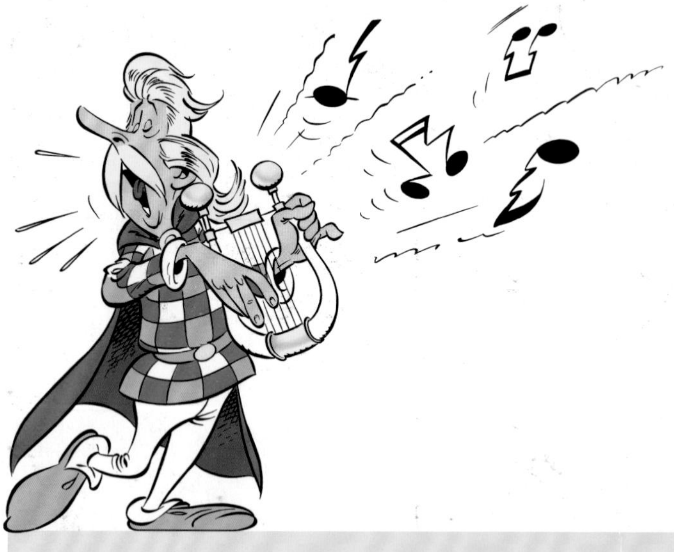

CACOFONIX, THE BARD. OPINION IS DIVIDED AS TO HIS MUSICAL GIFTS. CACOFONIX THINKS HE'S A GENIUS. EVERYONE ELSE THINKS HE'S UNSPEAKABLE. BUT SO LONG AS HE DOESN'T SPEAK, LET ALONE SING, EVERYBODY LIKES HIM . . .

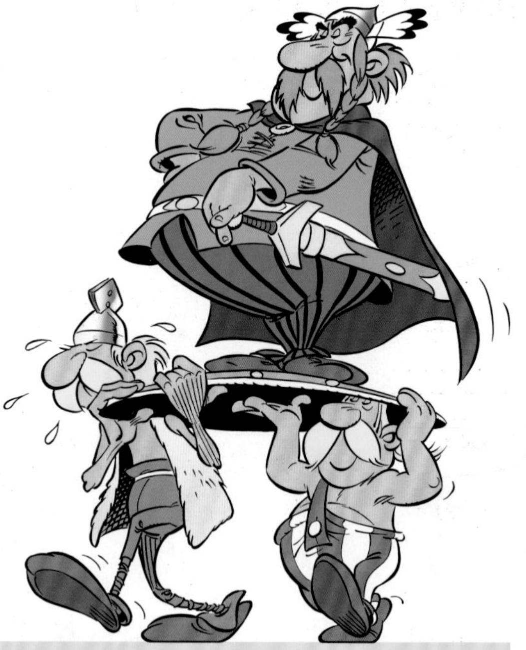

FINALLY, VITALSTATISTIX, THE CHIEF OF THE TRIBE. MAJESTIC, BRAVE AND HOT-TEMPERED, THE OLD WARRIOR IS RESPECTED BY HIS MEN AND FEARED BY HIS ENEMIES. VITALSTATISTIX HIMSELF HAS ONLY ONE FEAR, HE IS AFRAID THE SKY MAY FALL ON HIS HEAD TOMORROW. BUT AS HE ALWAYS SAYS, TOMORROW NEVER COMES.

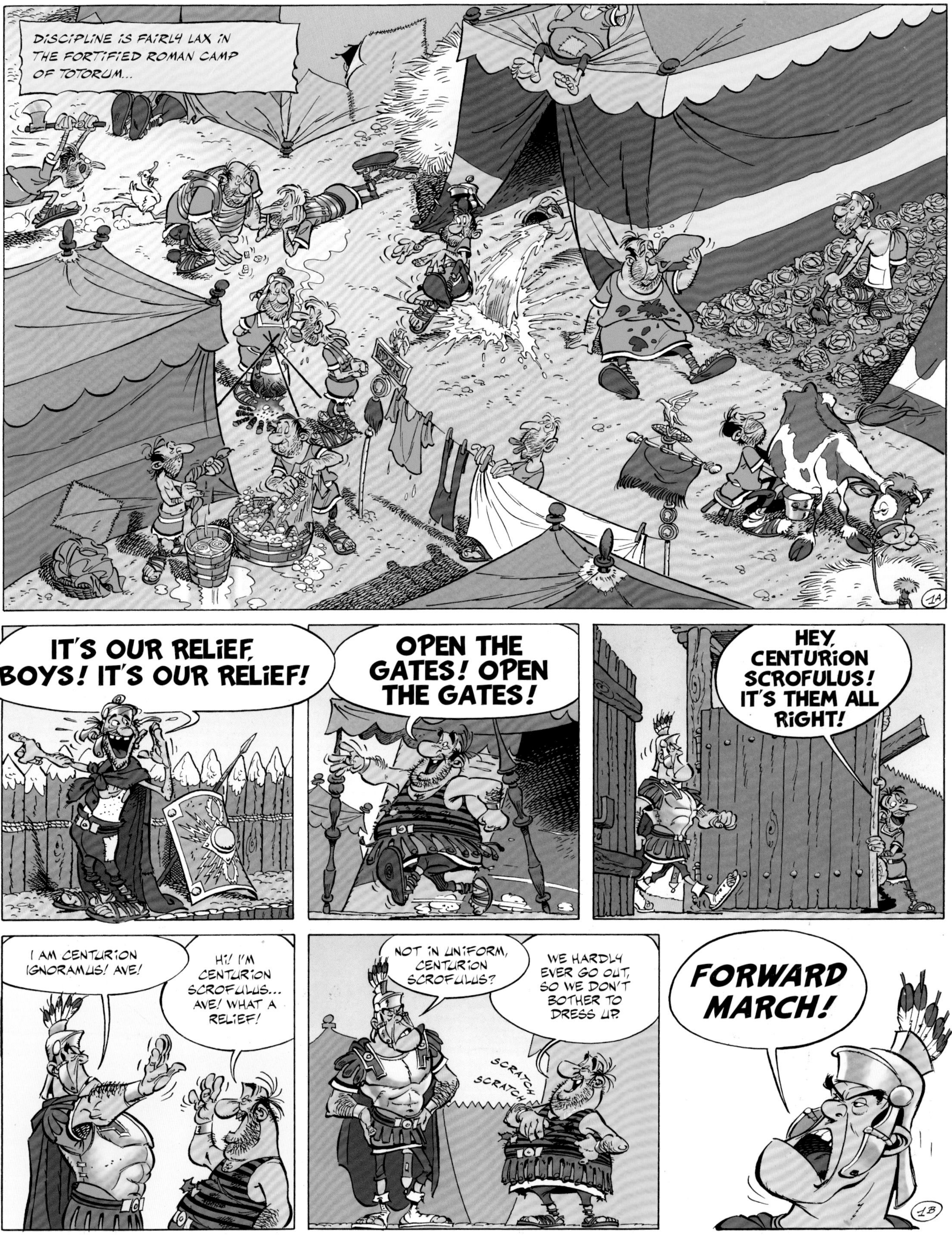
DISCIPLINE IS FAIRLY LAX IN THE FORTIFIED ROMAN CAMP OF TOTORUM...
IT'S OUR RELIEF, BOYS! IT'S OUR RELIEF!
OPEN THE GATES! OPEN THE GATES!
HEY, CENTURION SCROFULUS! IT'S THEM ALL RIGHT!
I AM CENTURION IGNORAMUS! AVE!
HI! I'M CENTURION SCROFULUS... AVE! WHAT A RELIEF!
NOT IN UNIFORM, CENTURION SCROFULUS?
WE HARDLY EVER GO OUT, SO WE DON'T BOTHER TO DRESS UP.
SCRATCH SCRATCH
FORWARD MARCH!

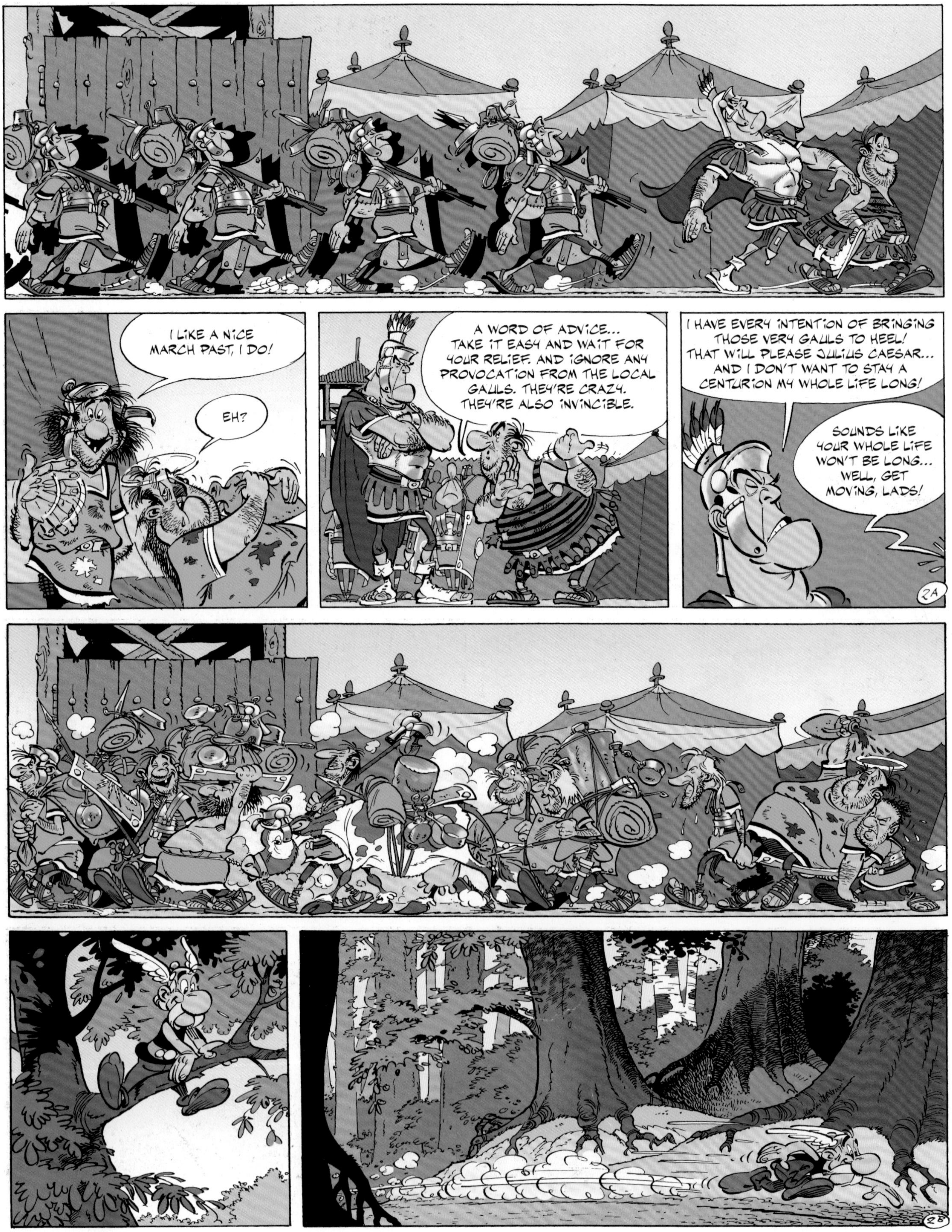
I LIKE A NICE MARCH PAST, I DO!
EH?
A WORD OF ADVICE... TAKE IT EASY AND WAIT FOR YOUR RELIEF. AND IGNORE ANY PROVOCATION FROM THE LOCAL GAULS. THEY'RE CRAZY. THEY'RE ALSO INVINCIBLE.
I HAVE EVERY INTENTION OF BRINGING THOSE VERY GAULS TO HEEL! THAT WILL PLEASE JULIUS CAESAR... AND I DON'T WANT TO STAY A CENTURION MY WHOLE LIFE LONG!
SOUNDS LIKE YOUR WHOLE LIFE WON'T BE LONG... WELL, GET MOVING, LADS!
2A
2B

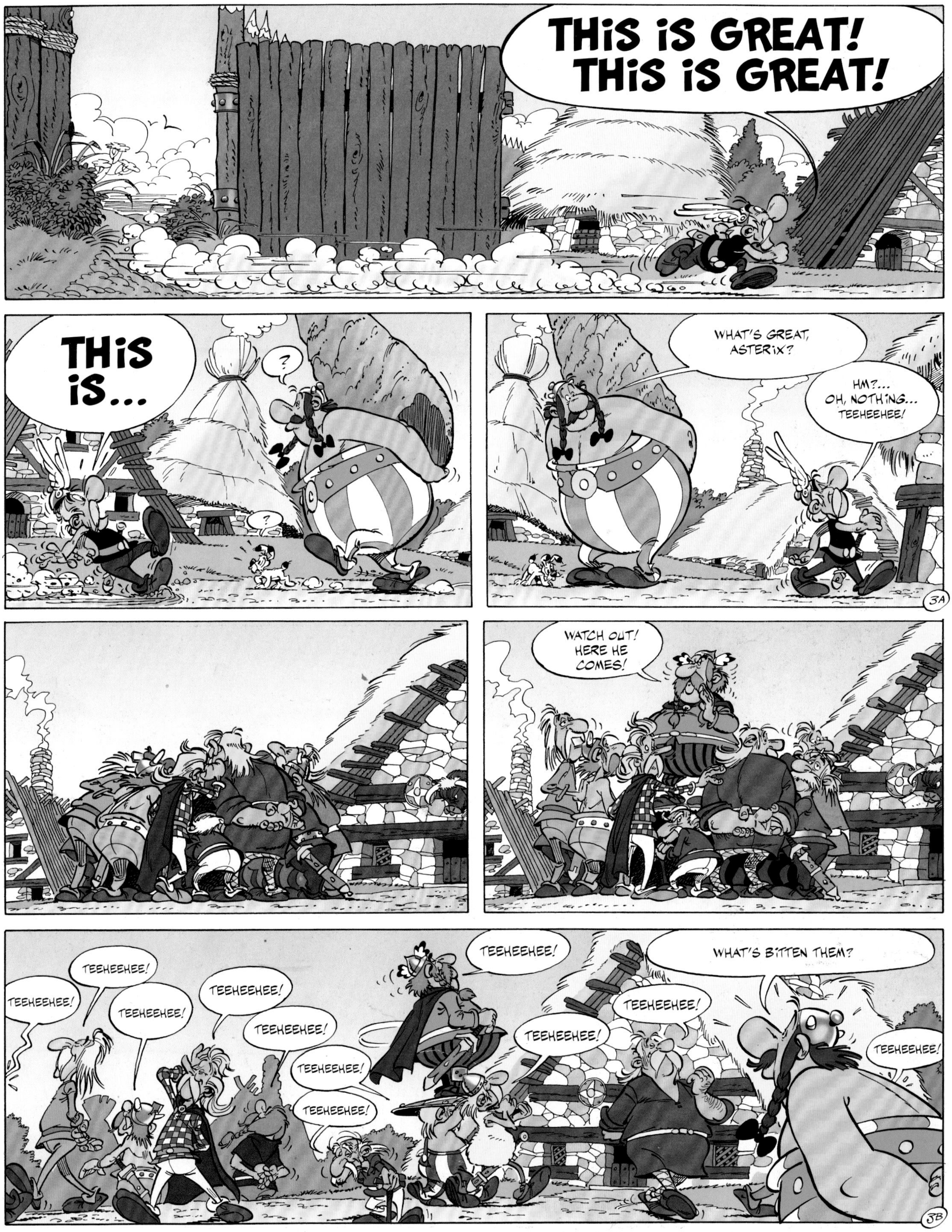
THIS IS GREAT! THIS IS GREAT!
THIS IS...
?
?
WHAT'S GREAT, ASTERIX?
HM?... OH, NOTHING... TEEHEEHEE!
WATCH OUT! HERE HE COMES!
TEEHEEHEE!
TEEHEEHEE!
TEEHEEHEE!
TEEHEEHEE!
TEEHEEHEE!
TEEHEEHEE!
TEEHEEHEE!
TEEHEEHEE!
TEEHEEHEE!
TEEHEEHEE!
WHAT'S BITTEN THEM?
TEEHEEHEE!

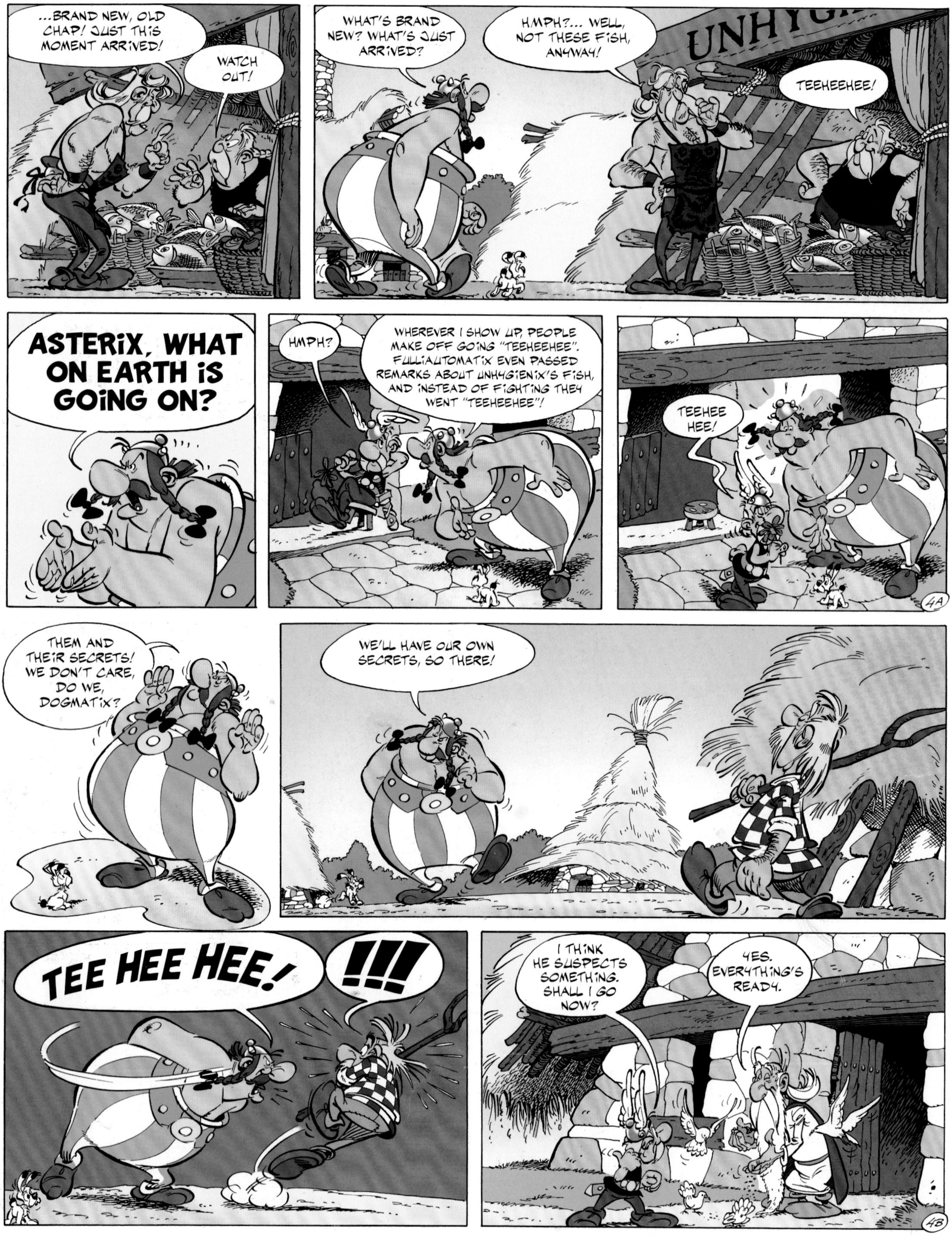

...BRAND NEW, OLD CHAP! JUST THIS MOMENT ARRIVED!
WATCH OUT!
WHAT'S BRAND NEW? WHAT'S JUST ARRIVED?
HMPH?... WELL, NOT THESE FISH, ANYWAY!
UNHYG
TEEHEEHEE!
ASTERIX, WHAT ON EARTH IS GOING ON?
HMPH?
WHEREVER I SHOW UP, PEOPLE MAKE OFF GOING "TEEHEEHEE". FULLIAUTOMATIX EVEN PASSED REMARKS ABOUT UNHYGIENIX'S FISH, AND INSTEAD OF FIGHTING THEY WENT "TEEHEEHEE"!
TEEHEE HEE!
THEM AND THEIR SECRETS! WE DON'T CARE, DO WE, DOGMATIX?
WE'LL HAVE OUR OWN SECRETS, SO THERE!
TEE HEE HEE!
!!!
I THINK HE SUSPECTS SOMETHING. SHALL I GO NOW?
YES. EVERYTHING'S READY.

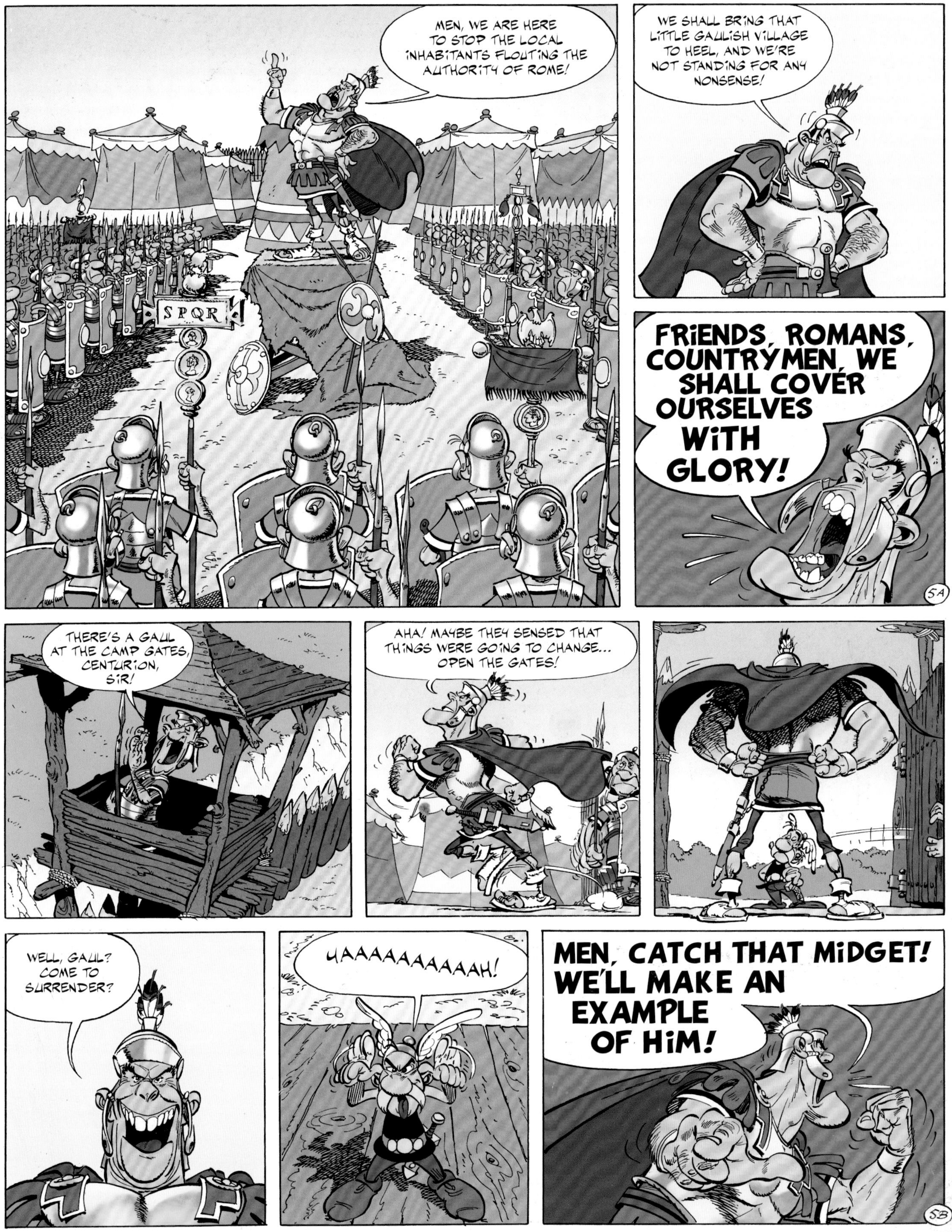
MEN, WE ARE HERE TO STOP THE LOCAL INHABITANTS FLOUTING THE AUTHORITY OF ROME!
SPQR
WE SHALL BRING THAT LITTLE GAULISH VILLAGE TO HEEL, AND WE'RE NOT STANDING FOR ANY NONSENSE!
FRIENDS, ROMANS, COUNTRYMEN, WE SHALL COVER OURSELVES WITH GLORY!
5A
THERE'S A GAUL AT THE CAMP GATES, CENTURION, SIR!
AHA! MAYBE THEY SENSED THAT THINGS WERE GOING TO CHANGE... OPEN THE GATES!
WELL, GAUL? COME TO SURRENDER?
YAAAAAAAAAAAH!
MEN, CATCH THAT MIDGET! WE'LL MAKE AN EXAMPLE OF HIM!
5B

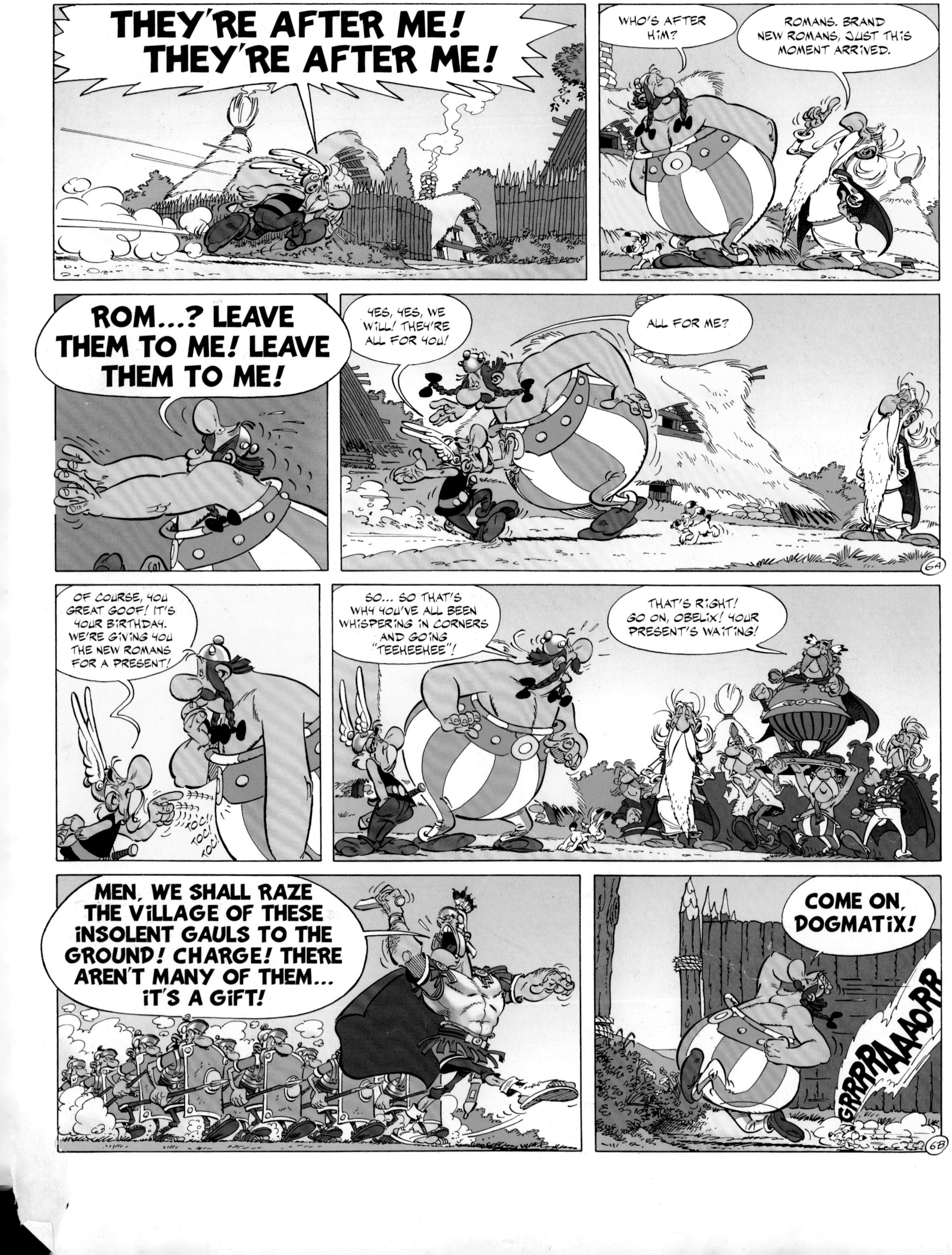
THEY'RE AFTER ME! THEY'RE AFTER ME!
WHO'S AFTER HIM?
ROMANS. BRAND NEW ROMANS, JUST THIS MOMENT ARRIVED.
ROM...? LEAVE THEM TO ME! LEAVE THEM TO ME!
YES, YES, WE WILL! THEY'RE ALL FOR YOU!
ALL FOR ME?
6A
OF COURSE, YOU GREAT GOOF! IT'S YOUR BIRTHDAY. WE'RE GIVING YOU THE NEW ROMANS FOR A PRESENT!
TOC! TOC! TOC!
SO... SO THAT'S WHY YOU'VE ALL BEEN WHISPERING IN CORNERS AND GOING "TEEHEEHEE"!
THAT'S RIGHT! GO ON, OBELIX! YOUR PRESENT'S WAITING!
MEN, WE SHALL RAZE THE VILLAGE OF THESE INSOLENT GAULS TO THE GROUND! CHARGE! THERE AREN'T MANY OF THEM... IT'S A GIFT!
COME ON, DOGMATIX!
GRRRRAAAORR
6B

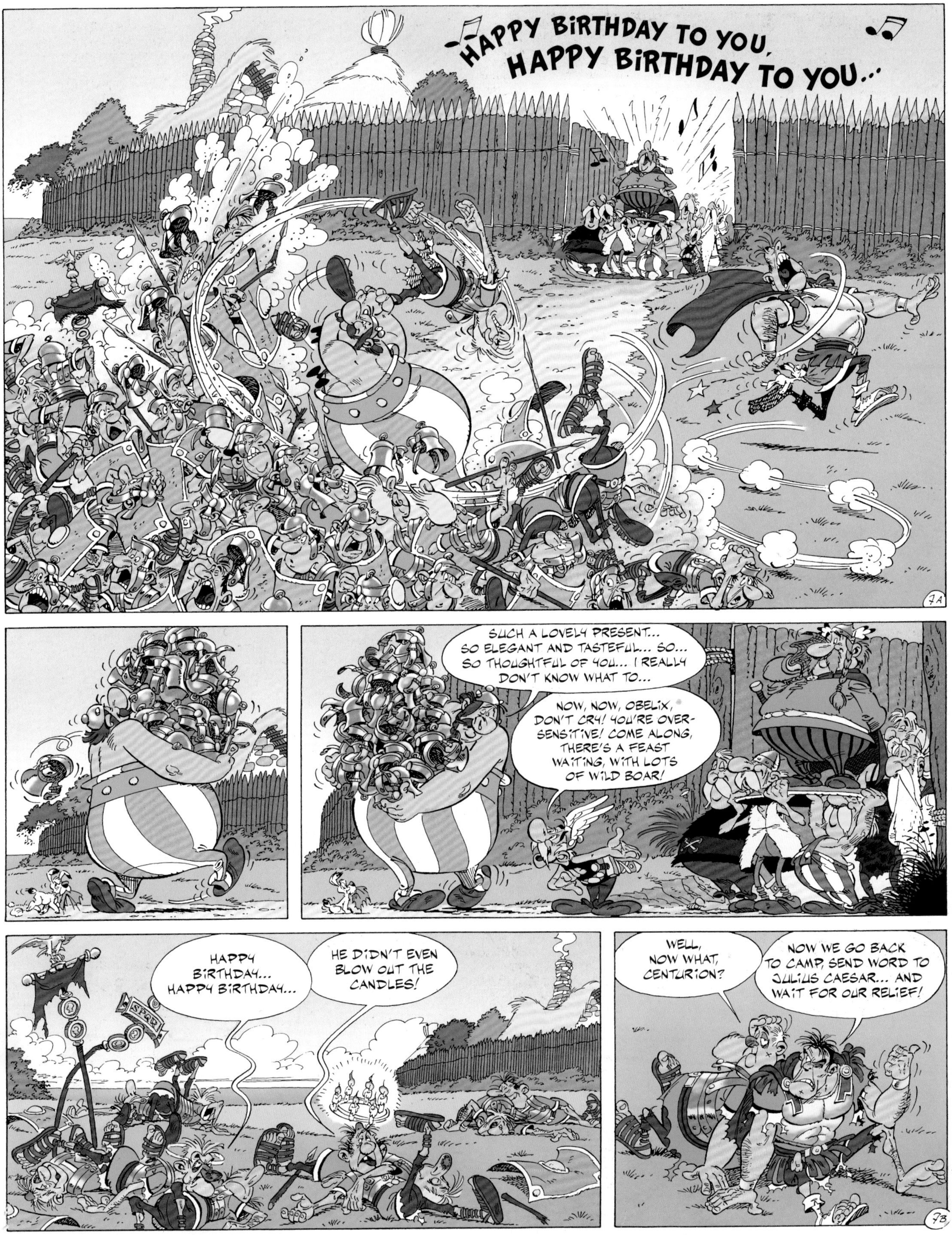
HAPPY BIRTHDAY TO YOU,
HAPPY BIRTHDAY TO YOU...
SUCH A LOVELY PRESENT... SO ELEGANT AND TASTEFUL... SO... SO THOUGHTFUL OF YOU... I REALLY DON'T KNOW WHAT TO...
NOW, NOW, OBELIX, DON'T CRY! YOU'RE OVER-SENSITIVE! COME ALONG, THERE'S A FEAST WAITING, WITH LOTS OF WILD BOAR!
HAPPY BIRTHDAY... HAPPY BIRTHDAY...
HE DIDN'T EVEN BLOW OUT THE CANDLES!
WELL, NOW WHAT, CENTURION?
NOW WE GO BACK TO CAMP, SEND WORD TO JULIUS CAESAR... AND WAIT FOR OUR RELIEF!

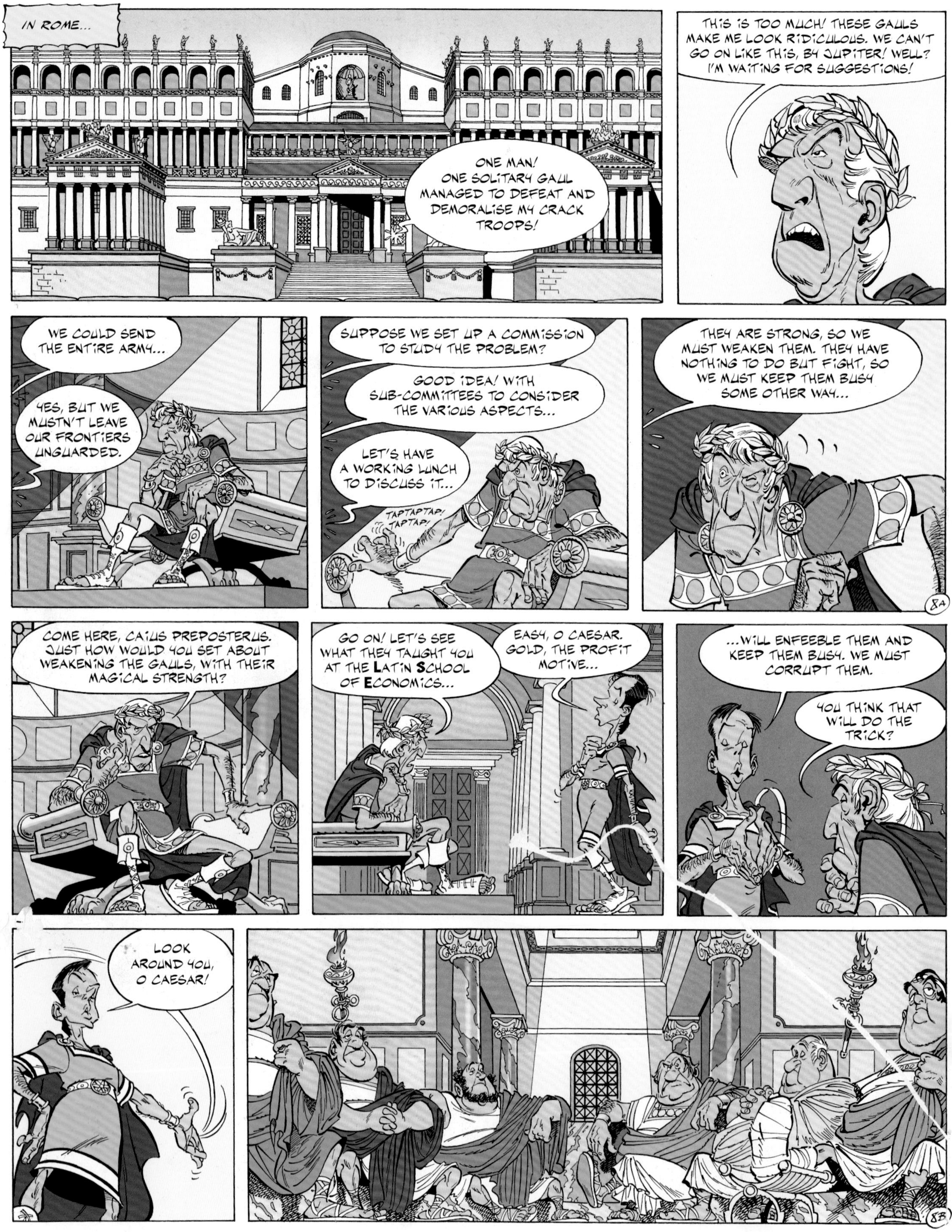
IN ROME...
ONE MAN! ONE SOLITARY GAUL MANAGED TO DEFEAT AND DEMORALISE MY CRACK TROOPS!
THIS IS TOO MUCH! THESE GAULS MAKE ME LOOK RIDICULOUS. WE CAN'T GO ON LIKE THIS, BY JUPITER! WELL? I'M WAITING FOR SUGGESTIONS!
WE COULD SEND THE ENTIRE ARMY...
YES, BUT WE MUSTN'T LEAVE OUR FRONTIERS UNGUARDED.
SUPPOSE WE SET UP A COMMISSION TO STUDY THE PROBLEM?
GOOD IDEA! WITH SUB-COMMITTEES TO CONSIDER THE VARIOUS ASPECTS...
LET'S HAVE A WORKING LUNCH TO DISCUSS IT...
TAPTAPTAP! TAPTAP!
THEY ARE STRONG, SO WE MUST WEAKEN THEM. THEY HAVE NOTHING TO DO BUT FIGHT, SO WE MUST KEEP THEM BUSY SOME OTHER WAY...
COME HERE, CAIUS PREPOSTERUS. JUST HOW WOULD YOU SET ABOUT WEAKENING THE GAULS, WITH THEIR MAGICAL STRENGTH?
GO ON! LET'S SEE WHAT THEY TAUGHT YOU AT THE LATIN SCHOOL OF ECONOMICS...
EASY, O CAESAR. GOLD, THE PROFIT MOTIVE...
...WILL ENFEEBLE THEM AND KEEP THEM BUSY. WE MUST CORRUPT THEM.
YOU THINK THAT WILL DO THE TRICK?
LOOK AROUND YOU, O CAESAR!

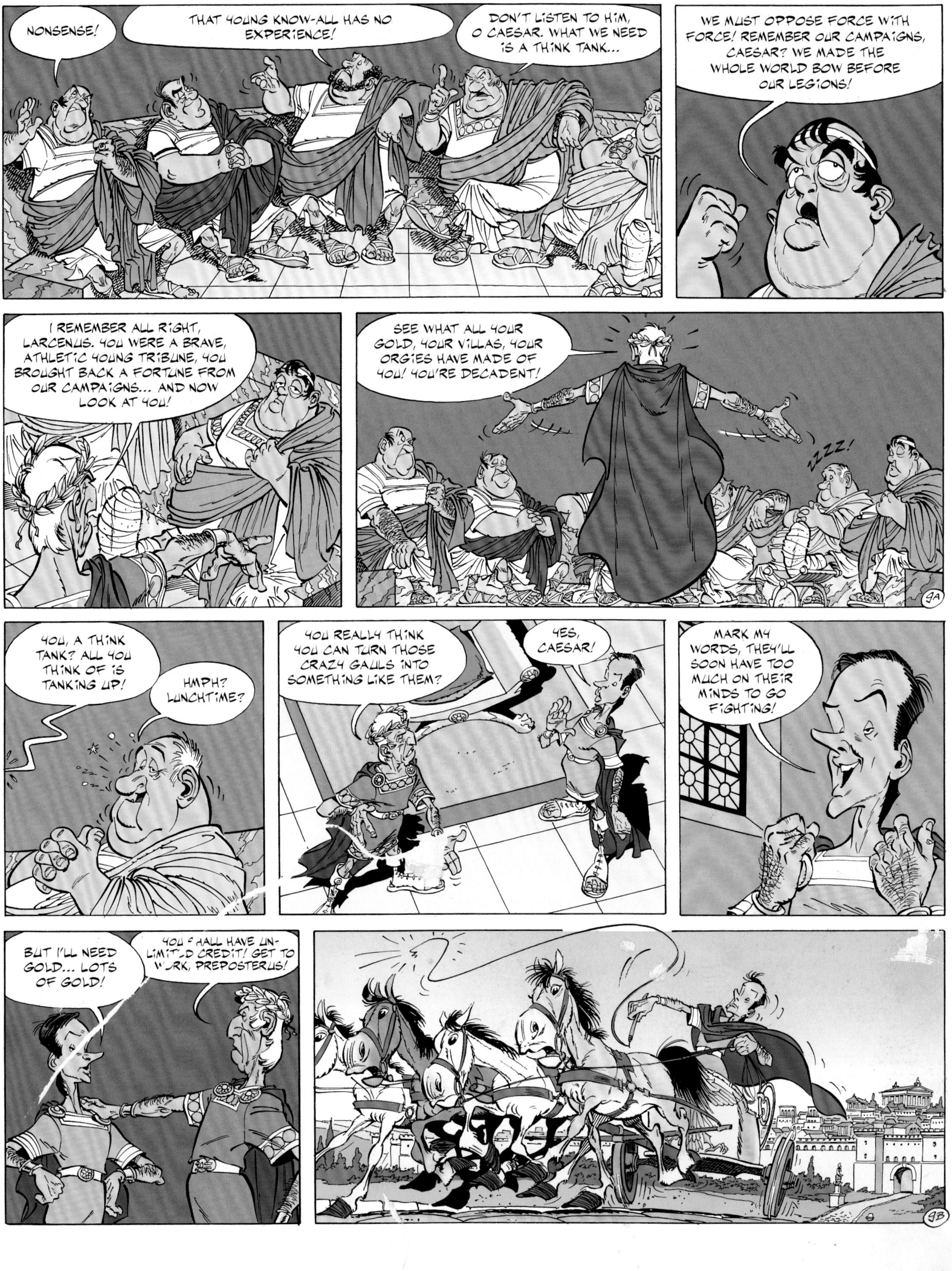

NONSENSE!
THAT YOUNG KNOW-ALL HAS NO EXPERIENCE!
DON'T LISTEN TO HIM, O CAESAR. WHAT WE NEED IS A THINK TANK...
WE MUST OPPOSE FORCE WITH FORCE! REMEMBER OUR CAMPAIGNS, CAESAR? WE MADE THE WHOLE WORLD BOW BEFORE OUR LEGIONS!
I REMEMBER ALL RIGHT, LARCENUS. YOU WERE A BRAVE, ATHLETIC YOUNG TRIBUNE, YOU BROUGHT BACK A FORTUNE FROM OUR CAMPAIGNS... AND NOW LOOK AT YOU!
SEE WHAT ALL YOUR GOLD, YOUR VILLAS, YOUR ORGIES HAVE MADE OF YOU! YOU'RE DECADENT!
ZZZZ!
YOU, A THINK TANK? ALL YOU THINK OF IS TANKING UP!
HMPH? LUNCHTIME?
YOU REALLY THINK YOU CAN TURN THOSE CRAZY GAULS INTO SOMETHING LIKE THEM?
YES, CAESAR!
MARK MY WORDS, THEY'LL SOON HAVE TOO MUCH ON THEIR MINDS TO GO FIGHTING!
BUT I'LL NEED GOLD... LOTS OF GOLD!
YOU SHALL HAVE UNLIMITED CREDIT! GET TO WORK, PREPOSTERUS!

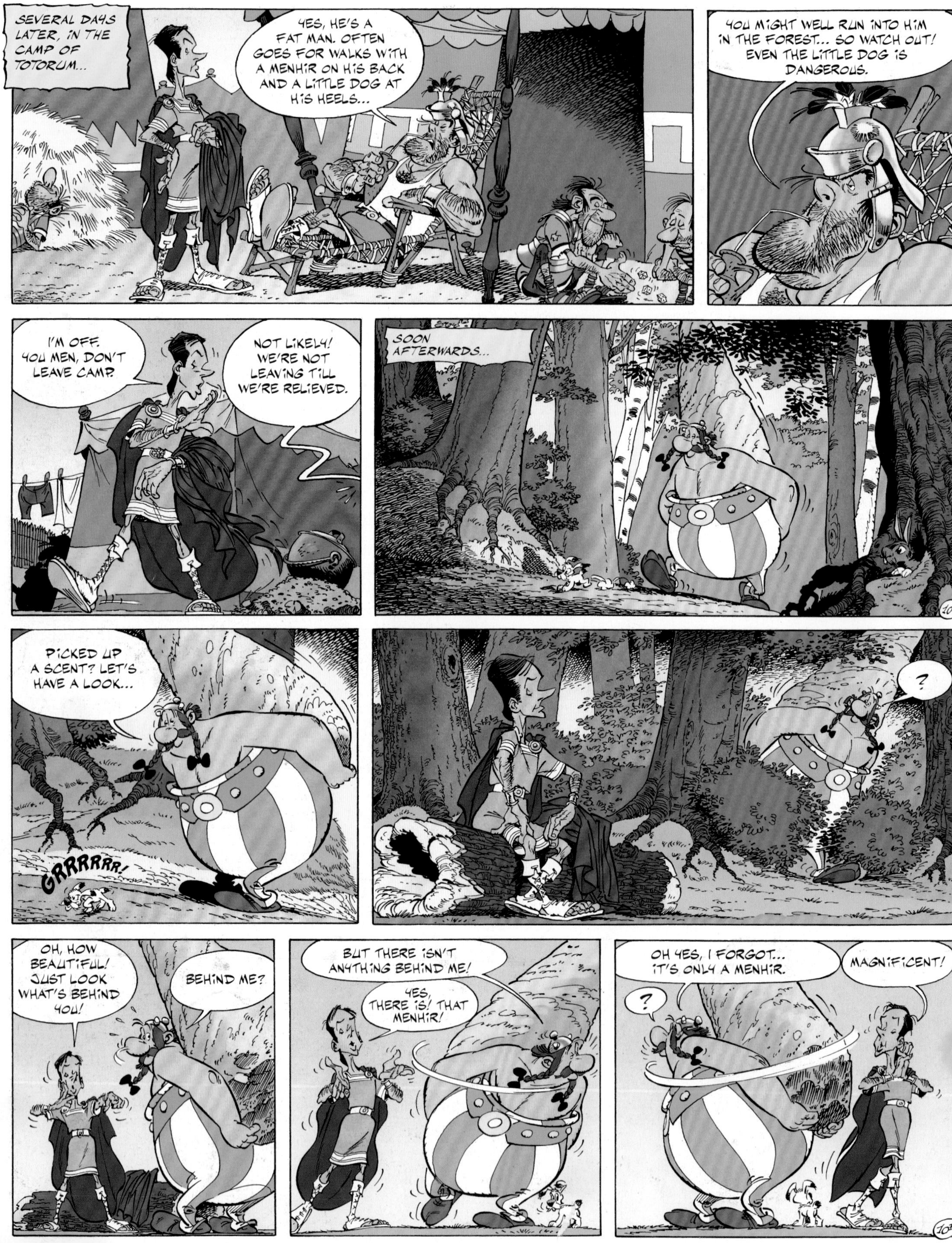
SEVERAL DAYS LATER, IN THE CAMP OF TOTORUM...
YES, HE'S A FAT MAN. OFTEN GOES FOR WALKS WITH A MENHIR ON HIS BACK AND A LITTLE DOG AT HIS HEELS...
YOU MIGHT WELL RUN INTO HIM IN THE FOREST... SO WATCH OUT! EVEN THE LITTLE DOG IS DANGEROUS.
I'M OFF. YOU MEN, DON'T LEAVE CAMP.
NOT LIKELY! WE'RE NOT LEAVING TILL WE'RE RELIEVED.
SOON AFTERWARDS...
PICKED UP A SCENT? LET'S HAVE A LOOK...
GRRRRRR!
?
OH, HOW BEAUTIFUL! JUST LOOK WHAT'S BEHIND YOU!
BEHIND ME?
BUT THERE ISN'T ANYTHING BEHIND ME!
YES, THERE IS! THAT MENHIR!
OH YES, I FORGOT... IT'S ONLY A MENHIR.
?
MAGNIFICENT!

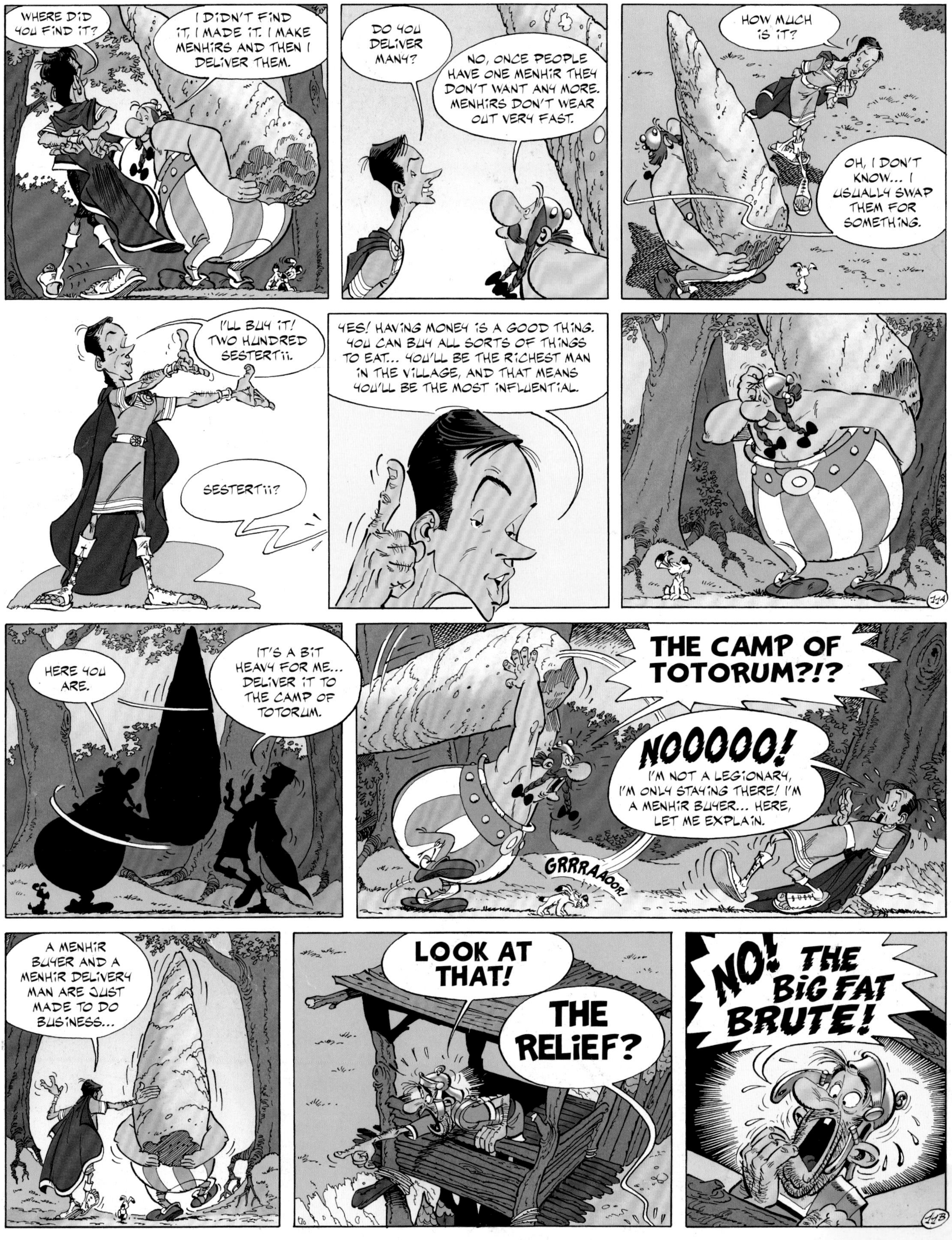

WHERE DID YOU FIND IT?
I DIDN'T FIND IT, I MADE IT. I MAKE MENHIRS AND THEN I DELIVER THEM.
DO YOU DELIVER MANY?
NO, ONCE PEOPLE HAVE ONE MENHIR THEY DON'T WANT ANY MORE. MENHIRS DON'T WEAR OUT VERY FAST.
HOW MUCH IS IT?
OH, I DON'T KNOW... I USUALLY SWAP THEM FOR SOMETHING.
I'LL BUY IT! TWO HUNDRED SESTERTII.
SESTERTII?
YES! HAVING MONEY IS A GOOD THING. YOU CAN BUY ALL SORTS OF THINGS TO EAT... YOU'LL BE THE RICHEST MAN IN THE VILLAGE, AND THAT MEANS YOU'LL BE THE MOST INFLUENTIAL.
HERE YOU ARE.
IT'S A BIT HEAVY FOR ME... DELIVER IT TO THE CAMP OF TOTORUM.
THE CAMP OF TOTORUM?!?
NOOOOO!
I'M NOT A LEGIONARY, I'M ONLY STAYING THERE! I'M A MENHIR BUYER... HERE, LET ME EXPLAIN.
GRRRAAOOR!
A MENHIR BUYER AND A MENHIR DELIVERY MAN ARE JUST MADE TO DO BUSINESS...
LOOK AT THAT!
THE RELIEF?
NO! THE BIG FAT BRUTE!

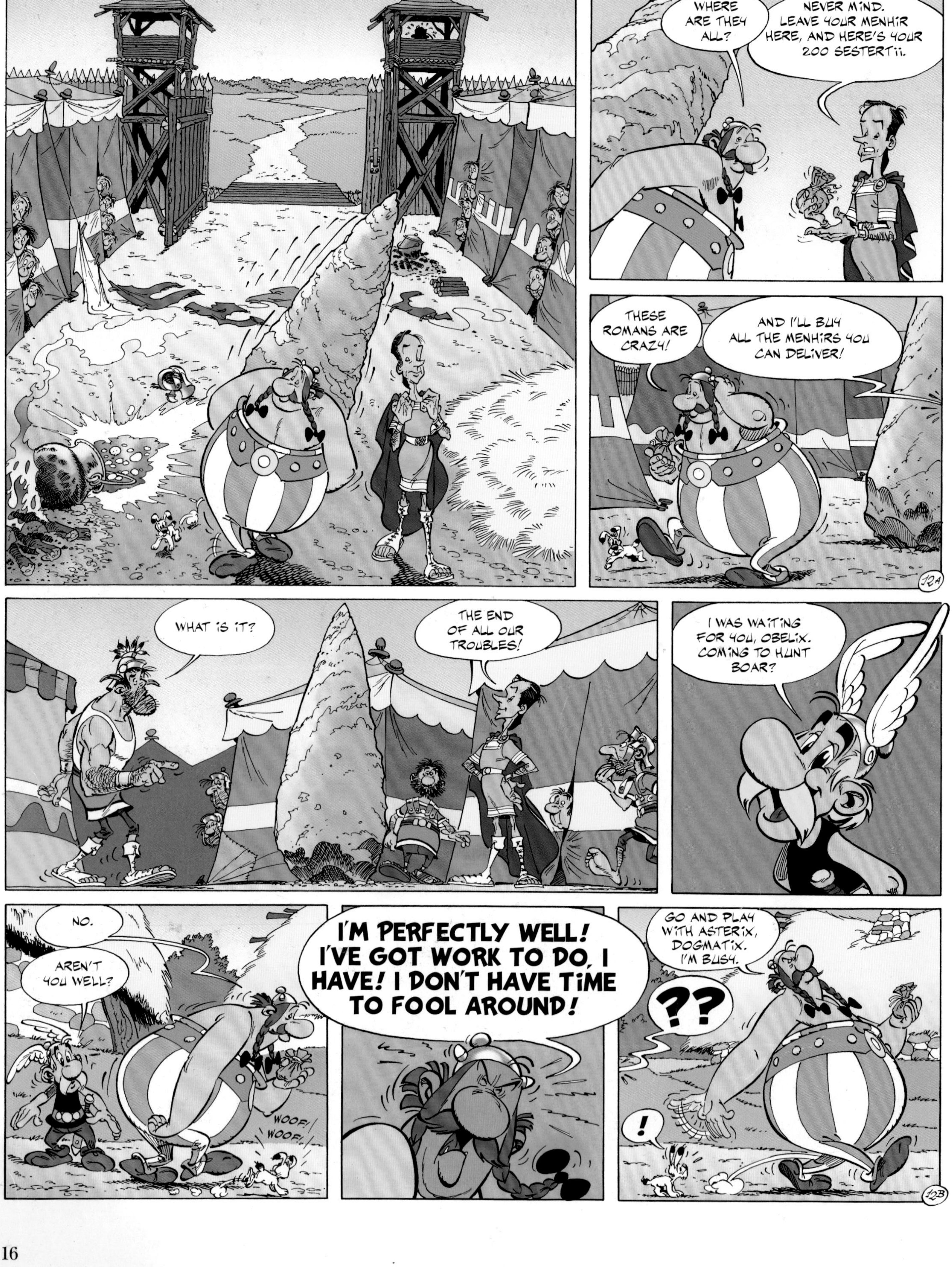

WHERE ARE THEY ALL?
NEVER MIND. LEAVE YOUR MENHIR HERE, AND HERE'S YOUR 200 SESTERTII.
THESE ROMANS ARE CRAZY!
AND I'LL BUY ALL THE MENHIRS YOU CAN DELIVER!
12A
WHAT IS IT?
THE END OF ALL OUR TROUBLES!
I WAS WAITING FOR YOU, OBELIX. COMING TO HUNT BOAR?
NO.
AREN'T YOU WELL?
WOOF! WOOF!
I'M PERFECTLY WELL! I'VE GOT WORK TO DO, I HAVE! I DON'T HAVE TIME TO FOOL AROUND!
GO AND PLAY WITH ASTERIX, DOGMATIX. I'M BUSY.
??
!
12B

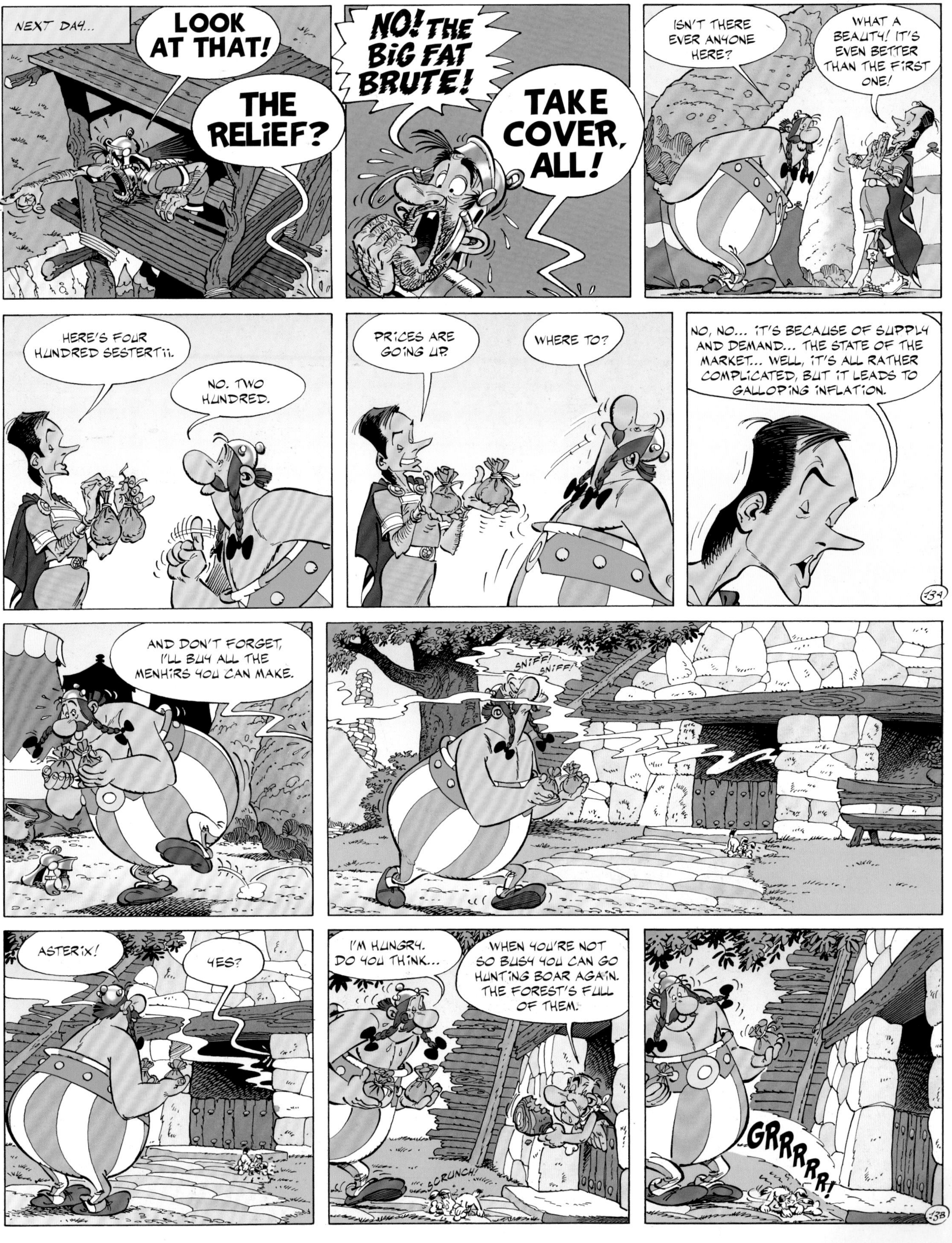

NEXT DAY...
LOOK AT THAT!
THE RELIEF?
NO! THE BIG FAT BRUTE!
TAKE COVER, ALL!
ISN'T THERE EVER ANYONE HERE?
WHAT A BEAUTY! IT'S EVEN BETTER THAN THE FIRST ONE!
HERE'S FOUR HUNDRED SESTERTII.
NO. TWO HUNDRED.
PRICES ARE GOING UP.
WHERE TO?
NO, NO... IT'S BECAUSE OF SUPPLY AND DEMAND... THE STATE OF THE MARKET... WELL, IT'S ALL RATHER COMPLICATED, BUT IT LEADS TO GALLOPING INFLATION.
AND DON'T FORGET, I'LL BUY ALL THE MENHIRS YOU CAN MAKE.
SNIFF! SNIFF!
ASTERIX!
YES?
I'M HUNGRY. DO YOU THINK...
WHEN YOU'RE NOT SO BUSY YOU CAN GO HUNTING BOAR AGAIN. THE FOREST'S FULL OF THEM.
SCRUNCH!
GRRRRRR!

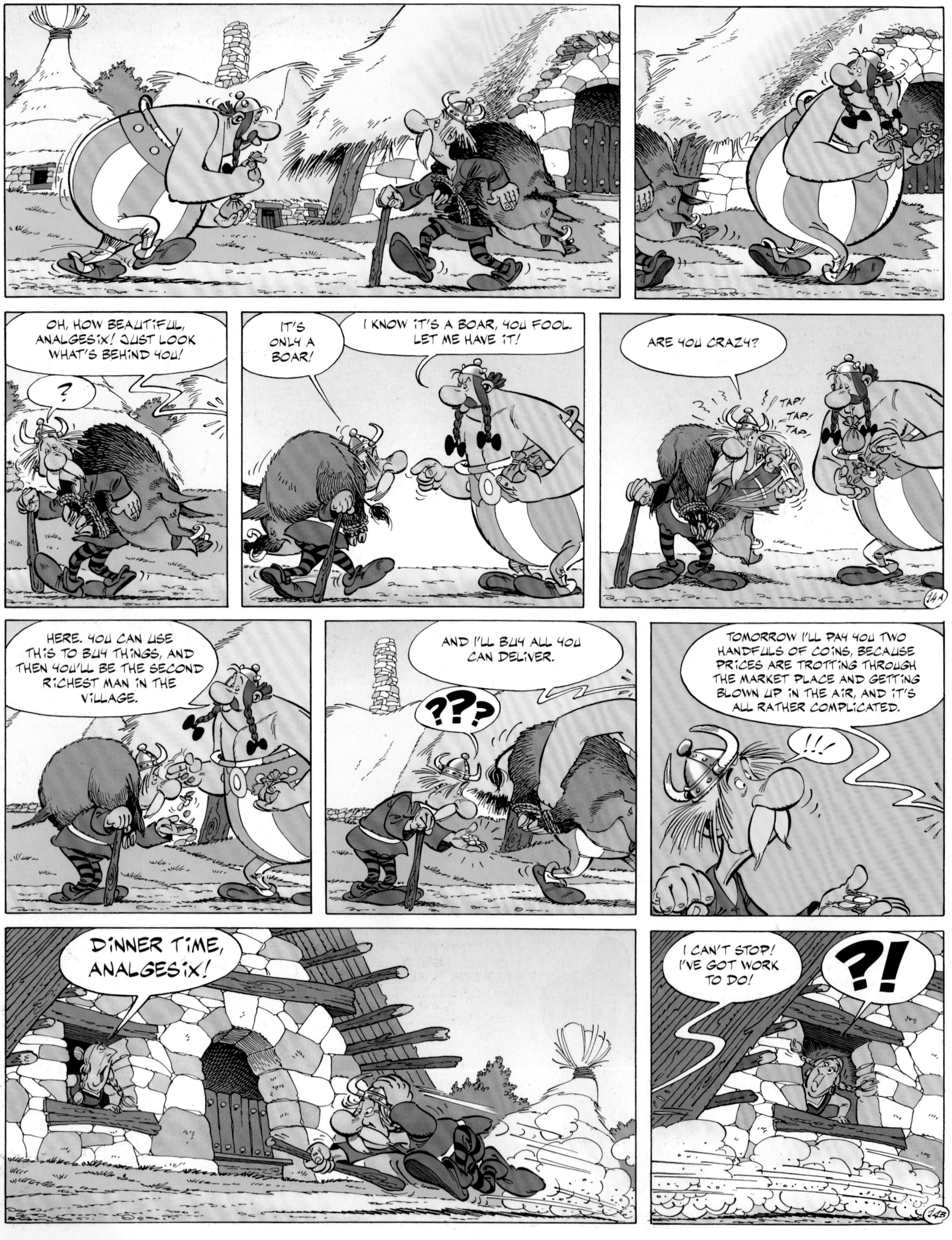
OH, HOW BEAUTIFUL, ANALGESIX! JUST LOOK WHAT'S BEHIND YOU!
?
IT'S ONLY A BOAR!
I KNOW IT'S A BOAR, YOU FOOL. LET ME HAVE IT!
ARE YOU CRAZY?
TAP! TAP! TAP!
HERE. YOU CAN USE THIS TO BUY THINGS, AND THEN YOU'LL BE THE SECOND RICHEST MAN IN THE VILLAGE.
AND I'LL BUY ALL YOU CAN DELIVER.
???
TOMORROW I'LL PAY YOU TWO HANDFULS OF COINS, BECAUSE PRICES ARE TROTTING THROUGH THE MARKET PLACE AND GETTING BLOWN UP IN THE AIR, AND IT'S ALL RATHER COMPLICATED.
!!!
DINNER TIME, ANALGESIX!
I CAN'T STOP! I'VE GOT WORK TO DO!
?!

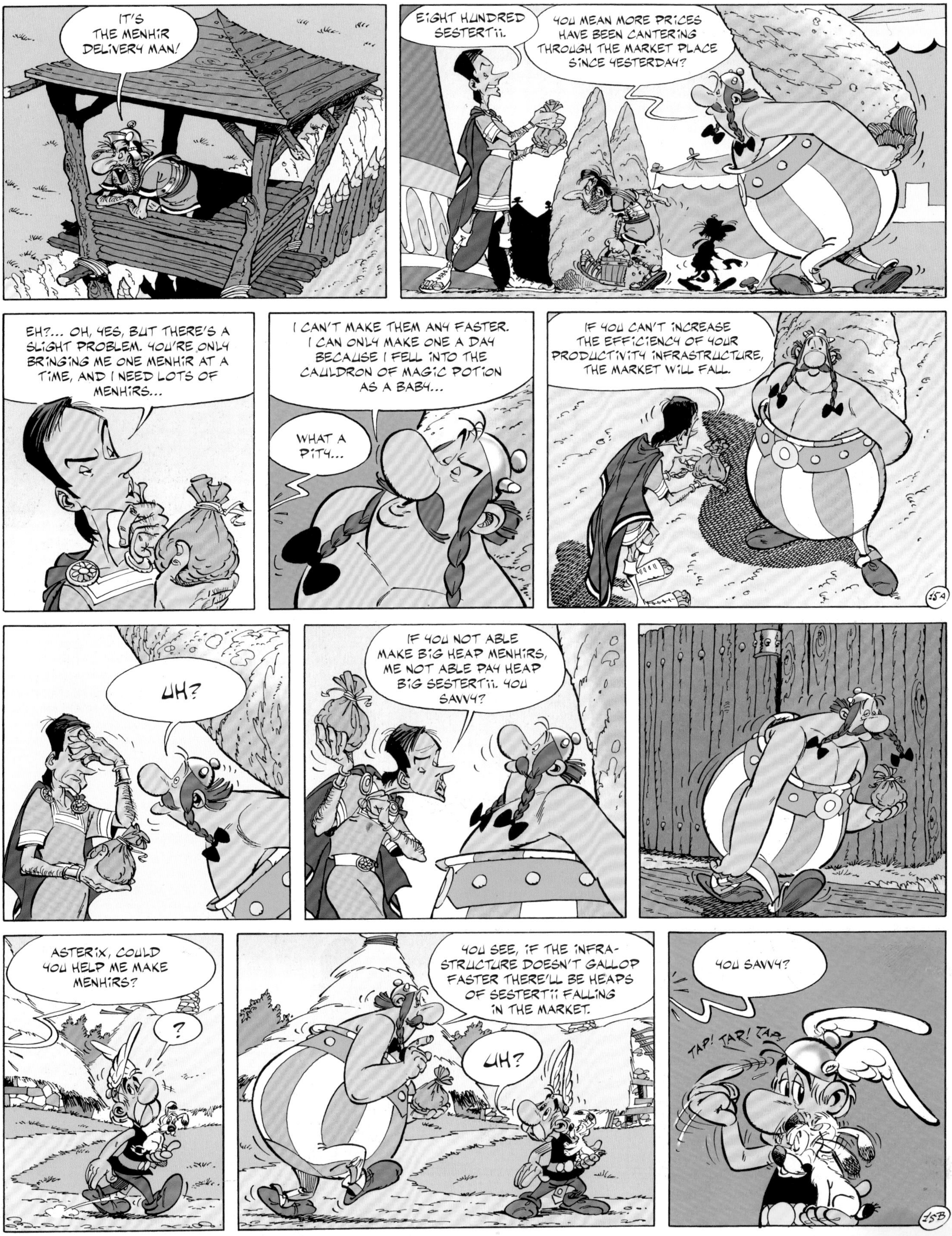

IT'S THE MENHIR DELIVERY MAN!
EIGHT HUNDRED SESTERTII.
YOU MEAN MORE PRICES HAVE BEEN CANTERING THROUGH THE MARKET PLACE SINCE YESTERDAY?
EH?... OH, YES, BUT THERE'S A SLIGHT PROBLEM. YOU'RE ONLY BRINGING ME ONE MENHIR AT A TIME, AND I NEED LOTS OF MENHIRS...
I CAN'T MAKE THEM ANY FASTER. I CAN ONLY MAKE ONE A DAY BECAUSE I FELL INTO THE CAULDRON OF MAGIC POTION AS A BABY...
WHAT A PITY...
IF YOU CAN'T INCREASE THE EFFICIENCY OF YOUR PRODUCTIVITY INFRASTRUCTURE, THE MARKET WILL FALL.
UH?
IF YOU NOT ABLE MAKE BIG HEAP MENHIRS, ME NOT ABLE PAY HEAP BIG SESTERTII. YOU SAVVY?
ASTERIX, COULD YOU HELP ME MAKE MENHIRS?
?
YOU SEE, IF THE INFRA-STRUCTURE DOESN'T GALLOP FASTER THERE'LL BE HEAPS OF SESTERTII FALLING IN THE MARKET.
UH?
YOU SAVVY?
TAP! TAP! TAP!

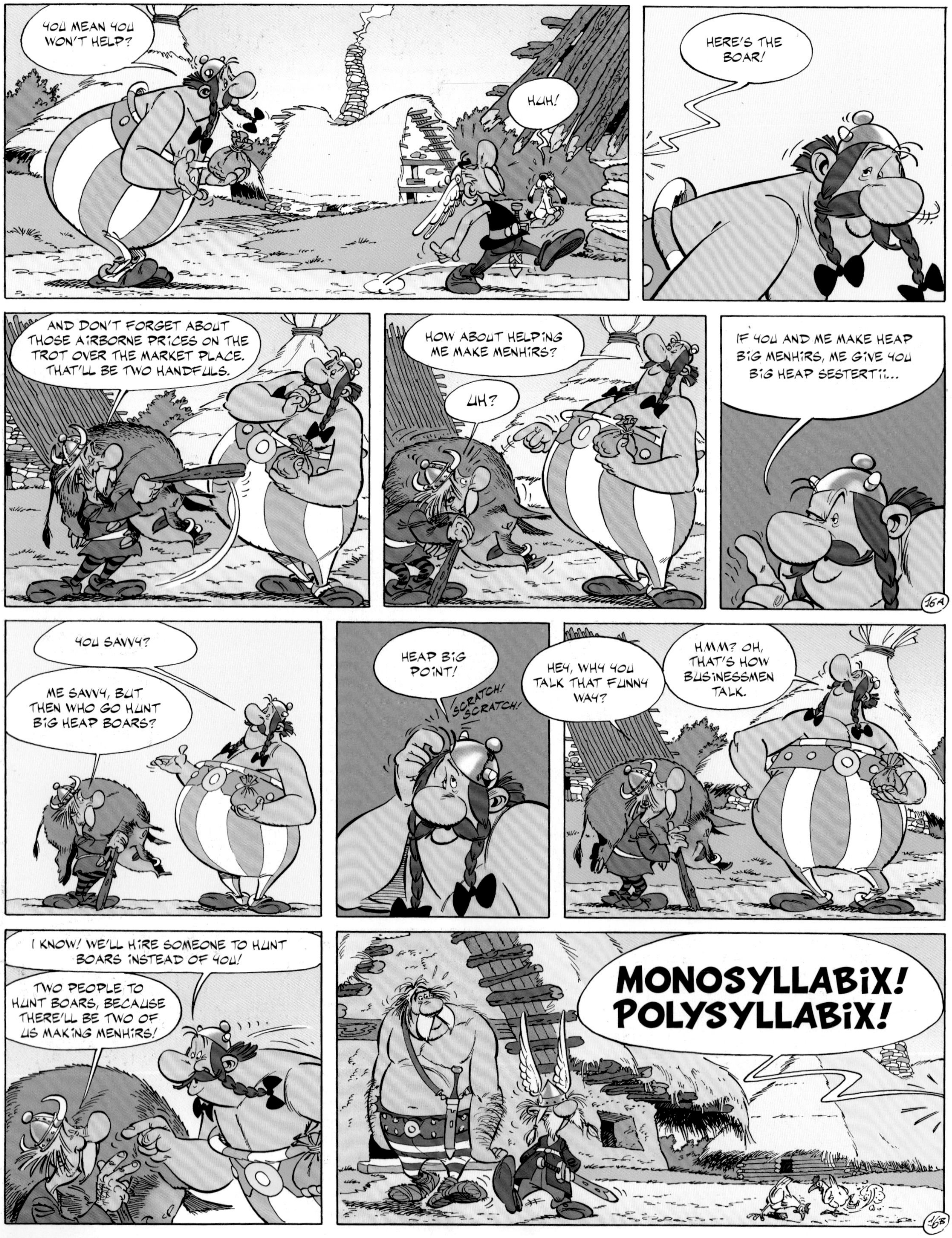
YOU MEAN YOU WON'T HELP?
HUH!
HERE'S THE BOAR!
AND DON'T FORGET ABOUT THOSE AIRBORNE PRICES ON THE TROT OVER THE MARKET PLACE. THAT'LL BE TWO HANDFULS.
HOW ABOUT HELPING ME MAKE MENHIRS?
UH?
IF YOU AND ME MAKE HEAP BIG MENHIRS, ME GIVE YOU BIG HEAP SESTERTII...
YOU SAVVY?
ME SAVVY, BUT THEN WHO GO HUNT BIG HEAP BOARS?
HEAP BIG POINT!
SCRATCH! SCRATCH!
HEY, WHY YOU TALK THAT FUNNY WAY?
HMM? OH, THAT'S HOW BUSINESSMEN TALK.
I KNOW! WE'LL HIRE SOMEONE TO HUNT BOARS INSTEAD OF YOU!
TWO PEOPLE TO HUNT BOARS, BECAUSE THERE'LL BE TWO OF US MAKING MENHIRS!
MONOSYLLABIX! POLYSYLLABIX!

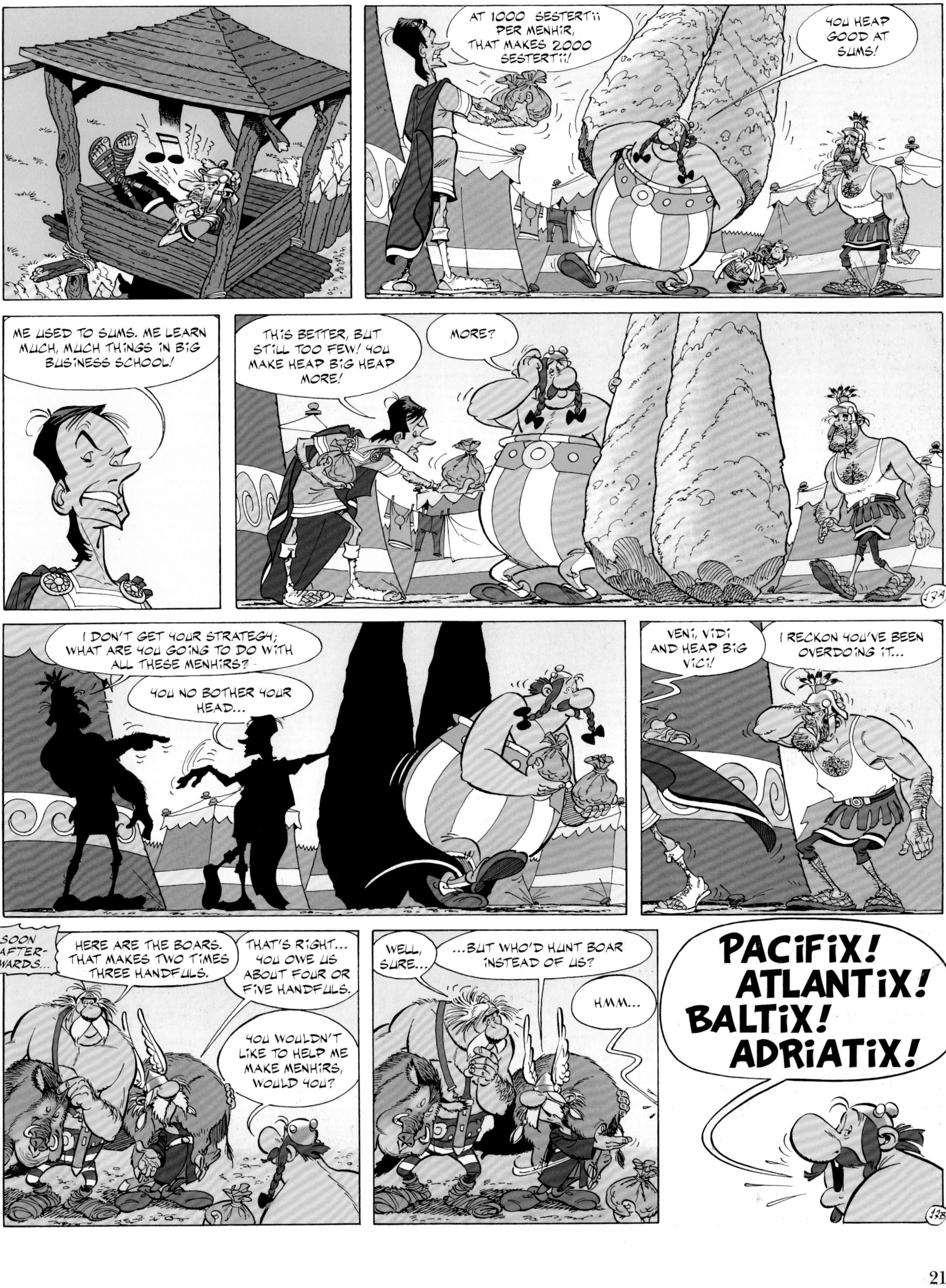
AT 1000 SESTERTII PER MENHIR, THAT MAKES 2000 SESTERTII!
YOU HEAP GOOD AT SUMS!
ME USED TO SUMS. ME LEARN MUCH, MUCH THINGS IN BIG BUSINESS SCHOOL!
THIS BETTER, BUT STILL TOO FEW! YOU MAKE HEAP BIG HEAP MORE!
MORE?
I DON'T GET YOUR STRATEGY; WHAT ARE YOU GOING TO DO WITH ALL THESE MENHIRS?
YOU NO BOTHER YOUR HEAD...
VENI, VIDI AND HEAP BIG VICI!
I RECKON YOU'VE BEEN OVERDOING IT...
SOON AFTERWARDS...
HERE ARE THE BOARS. THAT MAKES TWO TIMES THREE HANDFULS.
THAT'S RIGHT... YOU OWE US ABOUT FOUR OR FIVE HANDFULS.
YOU WOULDN'T LIKE TO HELP ME MAKE MENHIRS, WOULD YOU?
WELL, SURE...
...BUT WHO'D HUNT BOAR INSTEAD OF US?
HMM...
PACIFIX! ATLANTIX! BALTIX! ADRIATIX!

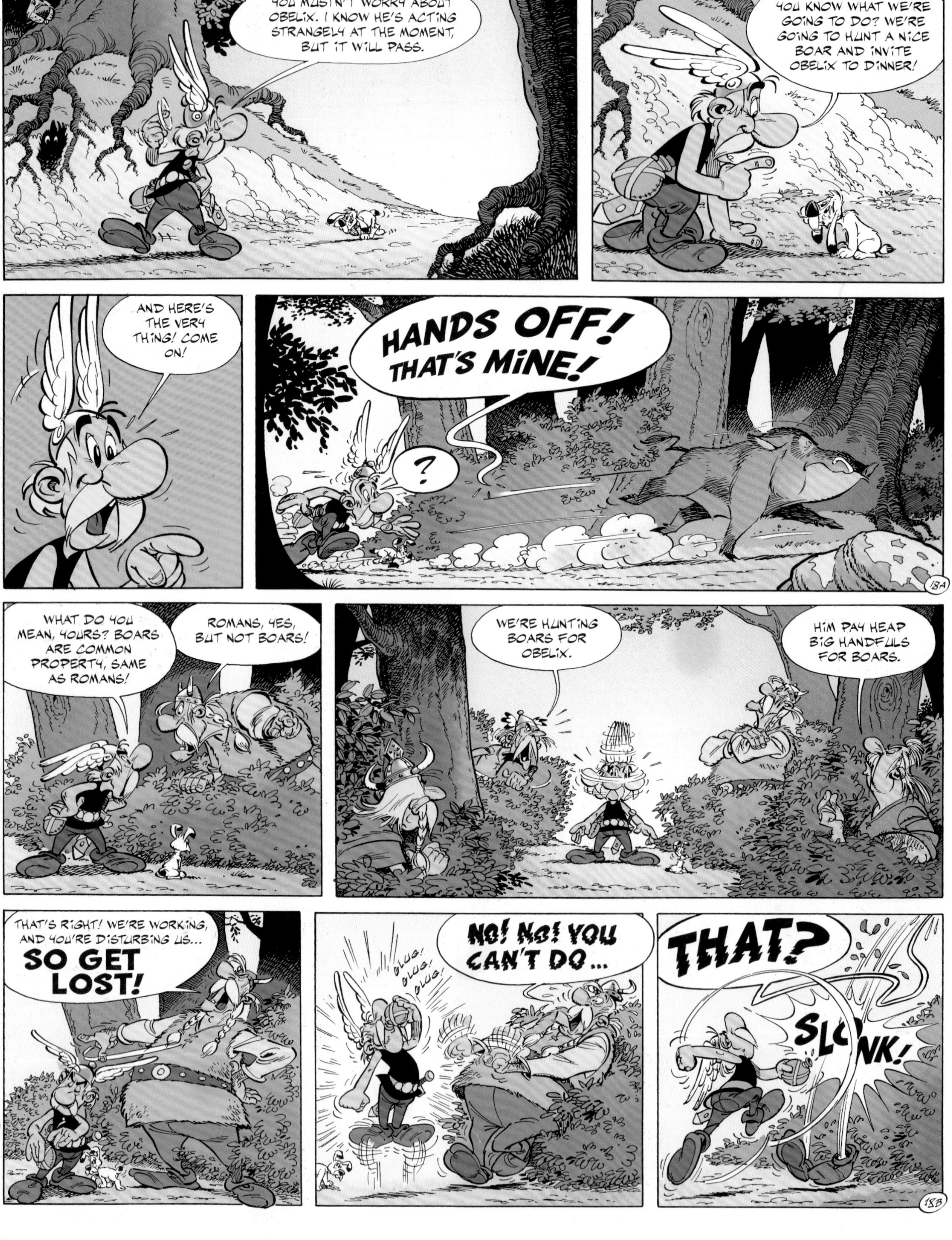
YOU MUSTN'T WORRY ABOUT OBELIX. I KNOW HE'S ACTING STRANGELY AT THE MOMENT, BUT IT WILL PASS.
YOU KNOW WHAT WE'RE GOING TO DO? WE'RE GOING TO HUNT A NICE BOAR AND INVITE OBELIX TO DINNER!
AND HERE'S THE VERY THING! COME ON!
HANDS OFF! THAT'S MINE!
?
18A
WHAT DO YOU MEAN, YOURS? BOARS ARE COMMON PROPERTY, SAME AS ROMANS!
ROMANS, YES, BUT NOT BOARS!
WE'RE HUNTING BOARS FOR OBELIX.
HIM PAY HEAP BIG HANDFULS FOR BOARS.
THAT'S RIGHT! WE'RE WORKING, AND YOU'RE DISTURBING US... SO GET LOST!
GLUG! GLUG! GLUG!
NO! NO! YOU CAN'T DO...
THAT?
SLONK!
18B

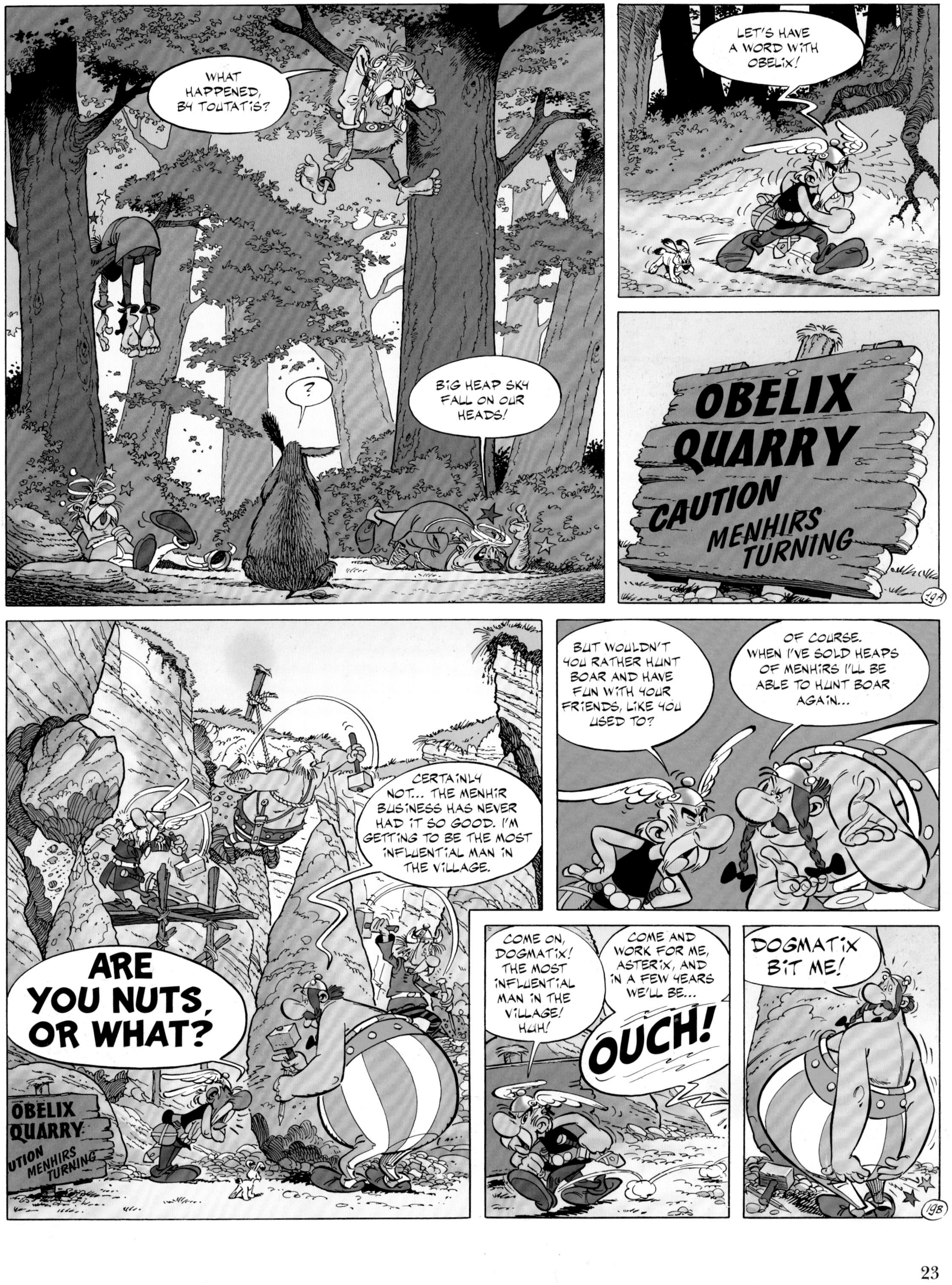
WHAT HAPPENED, BY TOUTATIS?
?
BIG HEAP SKY FALL ON OUR HEADS!
LET'S HAVE A WORD WITH OBELIX!
OBELIX QUARRY
CAUTION MENHIRS TURNING
ARE YOU NUTS, OR WHAT?
CERTAINLY NOT... THE MENHIR BUSINESS HAS NEVER HAD IT SO GOOD. I'M GETTING TO BE THE MOST INFLUENTIAL MAN IN THE VILLAGE.
OBELIX QUARRY
UTION MENHIRS TURNING
BUT WOULDN'T YOU RATHER HUNT BOAR AND HAVE FUN WITH YOUR FRIENDS, LIKE YOU USED TO?
OF COURSE. WHEN I'VE SOLD HEAPS OF MENHIRS I'LL BE ABLE TO HUNT BOAR AGAIN...
COME ON, DOGMATIX! THE MOST INFLUENTIAL MAN IN THE VILLAGE! HUH!
COME AND WORK FOR ME, ASTERIX, AND IN A FEW YEARS WE'LL BE...
OUCH!
DOGMATIX BIT ME!

I DON'T THINK IT'S ANYTHING SERIOUS...

BUT WHAT BOTHERS ME IS THIS SUDDEN PASSION THE ROMANS HAVE FOR MENHIRS...

NOT BAD GOING, BUT I MUST TALK TO YOU... I SUGGEST WE HAVE A WORKING LUNCH.

THAT'S LUCKY. SOMETHING SEEMS TO HAVE KEPT MY HUNTERS IN THE FOREST TODAY.

PRODUCTION HAS INCREASED, BUT YOU STILL HAVE A DELIVERY PROBLEM. YOU NEED TO STEP UP THE EFFICIENCY OF YOUR DISTRIBUTION CHANNELS.

UH?

SORRY, I FORGOT... YOU NOT BRING PLENTY MENHIRS ALL ONE TIME. YOU BRING MORE MENHIRS QUICK QUICK!

ME NOT FIND PLENTY DELIVERY MEN...

WELL, THINK THE PROBLEM OVER. WE'LL BE IN TOUCH AND HAVE ANOTHER WORKING LUNCH.

AND ANOTHER THING: YOU WANT TO START SPENDING YOUR SESTERTII. YOU NEED SOME SMARTER CLOTHES...

WHY? WHAT'S THE MATTER WITH MY BREECHES?

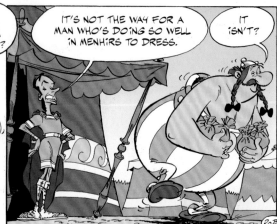

IT'S NOT THE WAY FOR A MAN WHO'S DOING SO WELL IN MENHIRS TO DRESS.

IT ISN'T?

24

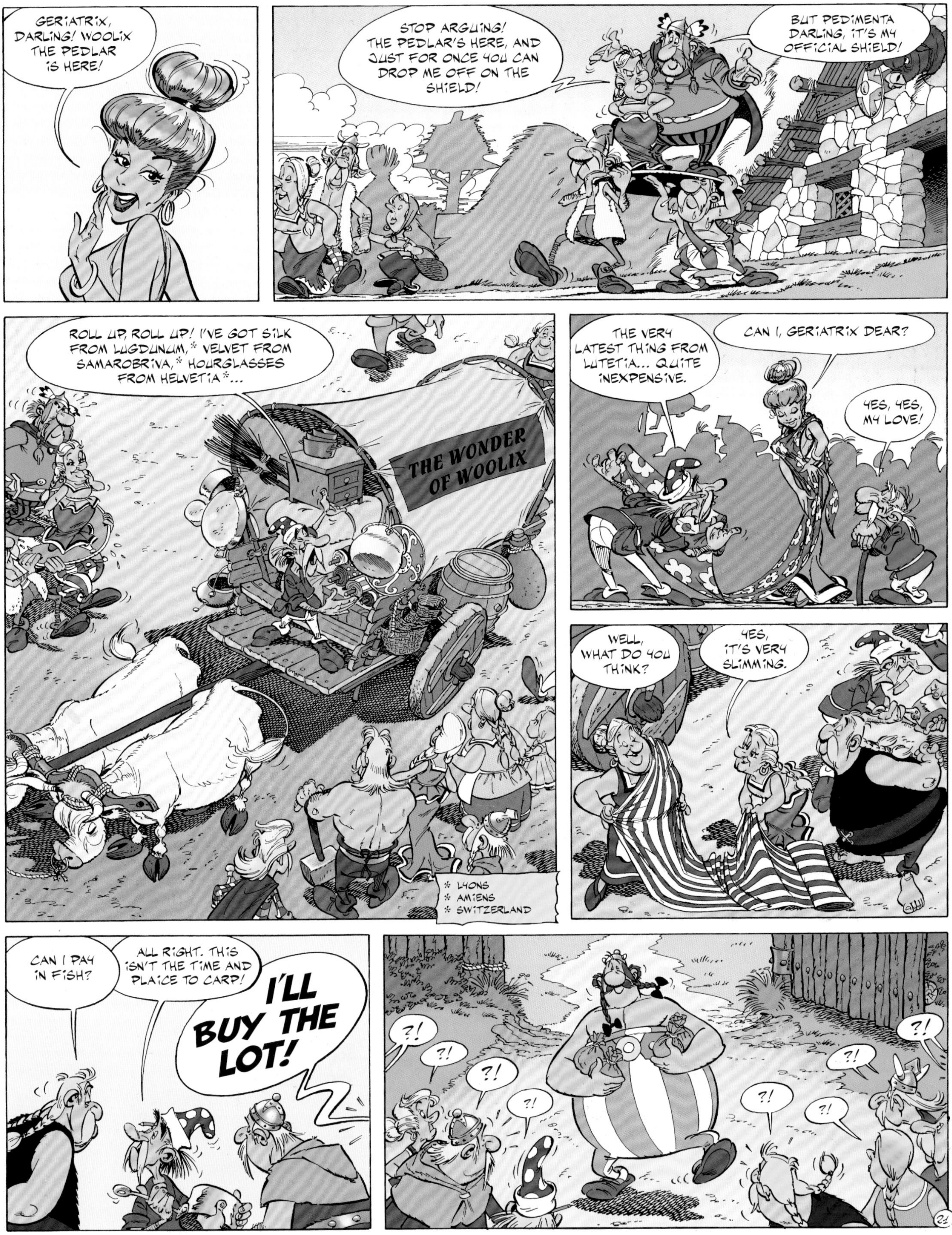
GERIATRIX, DARLING! WOOLIX THE PEDLAR IS HERE!
STOP ARGUING! THE PEDLAR'S HERE, AND JUST FOR ONCE YOU CAN DROP ME OFF ON THE SHIELD!
BUT PEDIMENTA DARLING, IT'S MY OFFICIAL SHIELD!
ROLL UP, ROLL UP! I'VE GOT SILK FROM LUGDUNUM,* VELVET FROM SAMAROBRIVA,* HOURGLASSES FROM HELVETIA*...
THE WONDER OF WOOLIX
* LYONS
* AMIENS
* SWITZERLAND
THE VERY LATEST THING FROM LUTETIA... QUITE INEXPENSIVE.
CAN I, GERIATRIX DEAR?
YES, YES, MY LOVE!
WELL, WHAT DO YOU THINK?
YES, IT'S VERY SLIMMING.
CAN I PAY IN FISH?
ALL RIGHT. THIS ISN'T THE TIME AND PLAICE TO CARP!
I'LL BUY THE LOT!
?!
?!
?!
?!
?!
?!
?!
?!
21

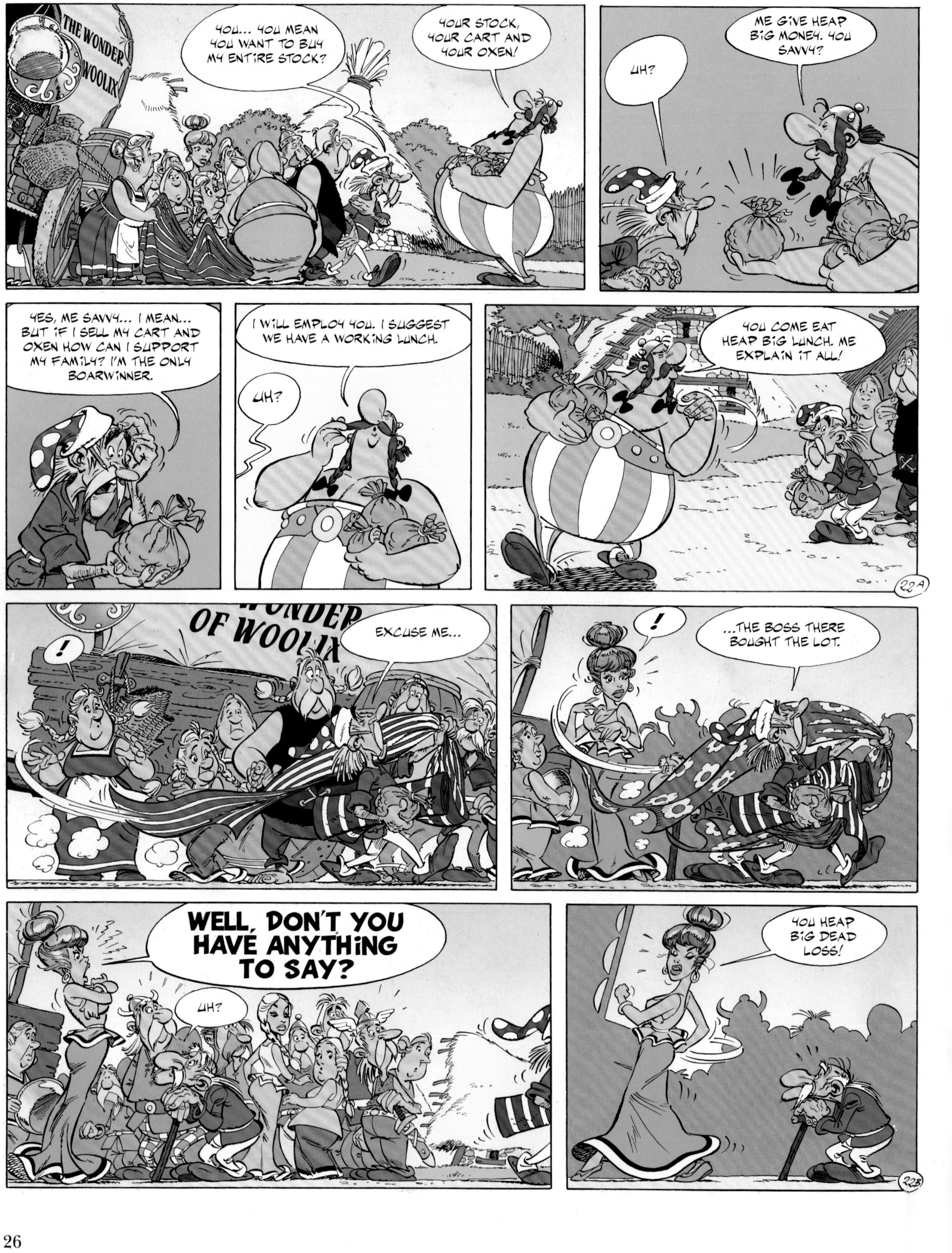
THE WONDER OF WOOLIX
YOU... YOU MEAN YOU WANT TO BUY MY ENTIRE STOCK?
YOUR STOCK, YOUR CART AND YOUR OXEN!
UH?
ME GIVE HEAP BIG MONEY. YOU SAVVY?
YES, ME SAVVY... I MEAN... BUT IF I SELL MY CART AND OXEN HOW CAN I SUPPORT MY FAMILY? I'M THE ONLY BOARWINNER.
I WILL EMPLOY YOU. I SUGGEST WE HAVE A WORKING LUNCH.
UH?
YOU COME EAT HEAP BIG LUNCH. ME EXPLAIN IT ALL!
!
EXCUSE ME...
!
...THE BOSS THERE BOUGHT THE LOT.
WELL, DON'T YOU HAVE ANYTHING TO SAY?
UH?
YOU HEAP BIG DEAD LOSS!

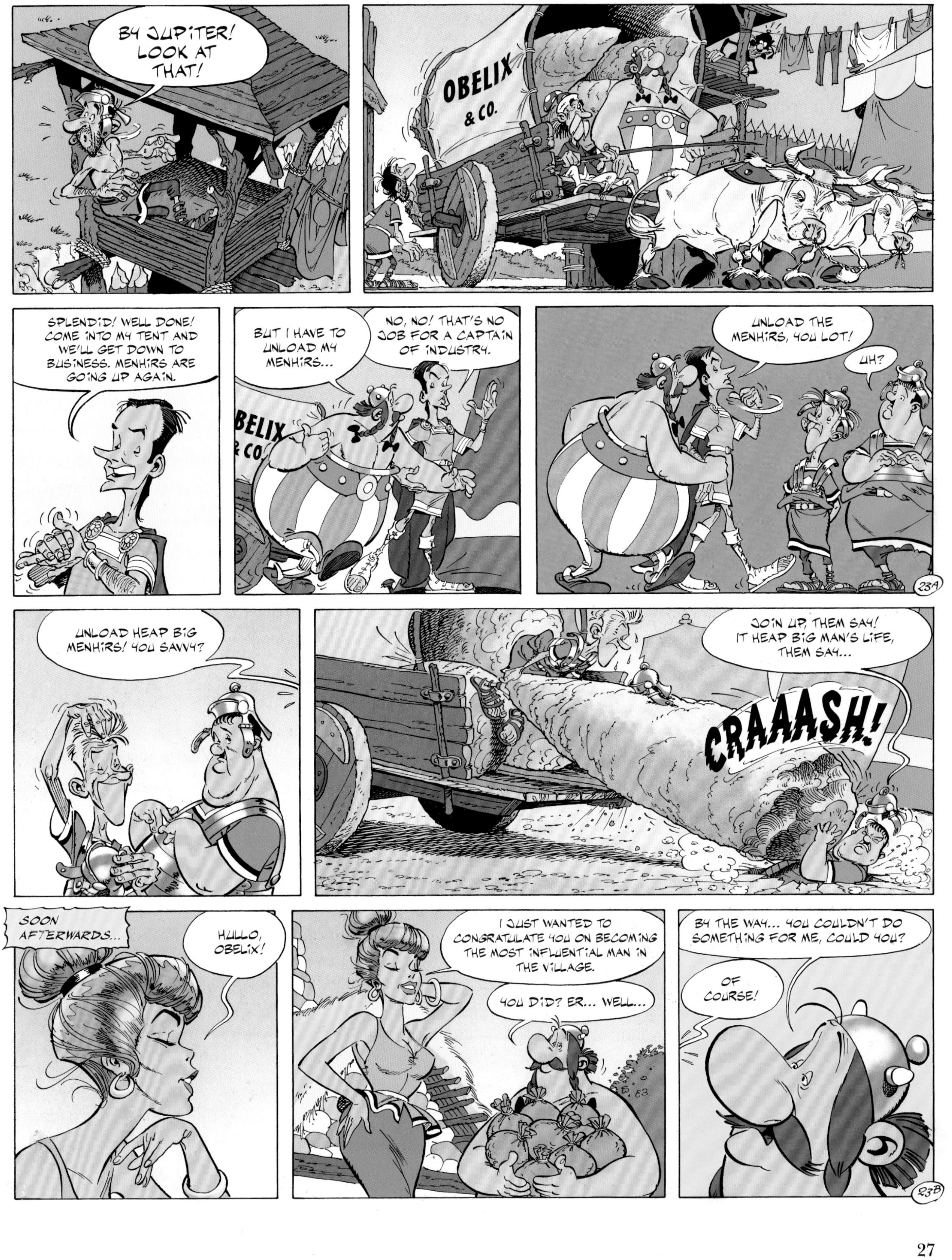
BY JUPITER! LOOK AT THAT!
OBELIX & CO.
SPLENDID! WELL DONE! COME INTO MY TENT AND WE'LL GET DOWN TO BUSINESS. MENHIRS ARE GOING UP AGAIN.
BUT I HAVE TO UNLOAD MY MENHIRS...
NO, NO! THAT'S NO JOB FOR A CAPTAIN OF INDUSTRY.
UNLOAD THE MENHIRS, YOU LOT!
UH?
UNLOAD HEAP BIG MENHIRS! YOU SAVVY?
JOIN UP, THEM SAY! IT HEAP BIG MAN'S LIFE, THEM SAY...
CRAAASH!
SOON AFTERWARDS...
HULLO, OBELIX!
I JUST WANTED TO CONGRATULATE YOU ON BECOMING THE MOST INFLUENTIAL MAN IN THE VILLAGE.
YOU DID? ER... WELL...
BY THE WAY... YOU COULDN'T DO SOMETHING FOR ME, COULD YOU?
OF COURSE!

POM TIDDLEY ♪ POM! ♪

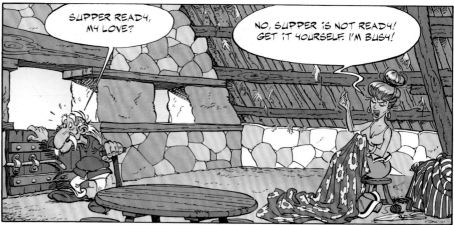

SUPPER READY, MY LOVE?

NO, SUPPER IS NOT READY! GET IT YOURSELF. I'M BUSY!

BUSY DOING WHAT, MY PET?

OBELIX ASKED ME TO MAKE HIM SOME CLOTHES. HE'S GOING TO PAY HANDSOMELY...

I HAVEN'T A THING TO WEAR! AND SINCE I CAN'T COUNT ON YOU, I HAVE TO FIND SOME WAY TO EARN A BIT OF MONEY!

24A

A LITTLE LATER...

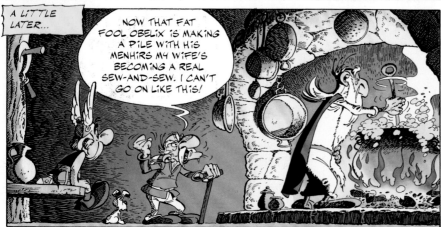

NOW THAT FAT FOOL OBELIX IS MAKING A PILE WITH HIS MENHIRS MY WIFE'S BECOMING A REAL SEW-AND-SEW. I CAN'T GO ON LIKE THIS!

CALM DOWN! AFTER ALL, OBELIX IS MY FRIEND!

WELL, MY WIFE IS MAKING EYES AT YOUR FRIEND!

AND SHE'S NEVER LOOKED AT ANYONE BUT ME... IT'S INCREDIBLE!

YES, I'VE OFTEN THOUGHT SO MYSELF...

SO WHAT AM I TO DO?

NOTHING. I'LL TRY TO TALK TO OBELIX!

YOU JUST DO THAT, OR I SHALL MAKE YOUR FINE FRIEND EAT MY STICK!

24B

28

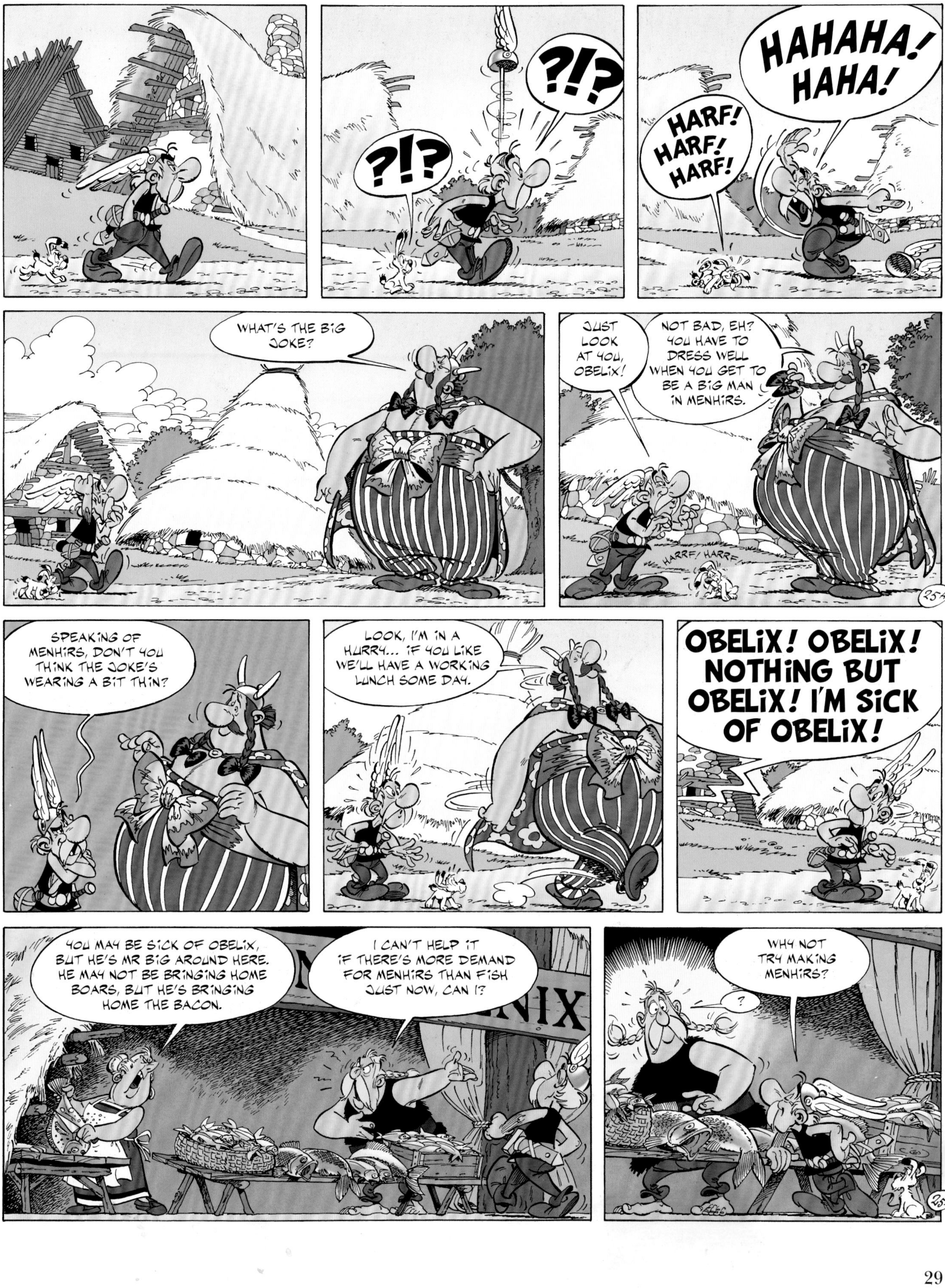
?!?
?!?
HAHAHA! HAHA!
HARF! HARF! HARF!
WHAT'S THE BIG JOKE?
JUST LOOK AT YOU, OBELIX!
NOT BAD, EH? YOU HAVE TO DRESS WELL WHEN YOU GET TO BE A BIG MAN IN MENHIRS.
HARRF! HARRF!
SPEAKING OF MENHIRS, DON'T YOU THINK THE JOKE'S WEARING A BIT THIN?
LOOK, I'M IN A HURRY... IF YOU LIKE WE'LL HAVE A WORKING LUNCH SOME DAY.
OBELIX! OBELIX! NOTHING BUT OBELIX! I'M SICK OF OBELIX!
YOU MAY BE SICK OF OBELIX, BUT HE'S MR BIG AROUND HERE. HE MAY NOT BE BRINGING HOME BOARS, BUT HE'S BRINGING HOME THE BACON.
I CAN'T HELP IT IF THERE'S MORE DEMAND FOR MENHIRS THAN FISH JUST NOW, CAN I?
NIX
?
WHY NOT TRY MAKING MENHIRS?

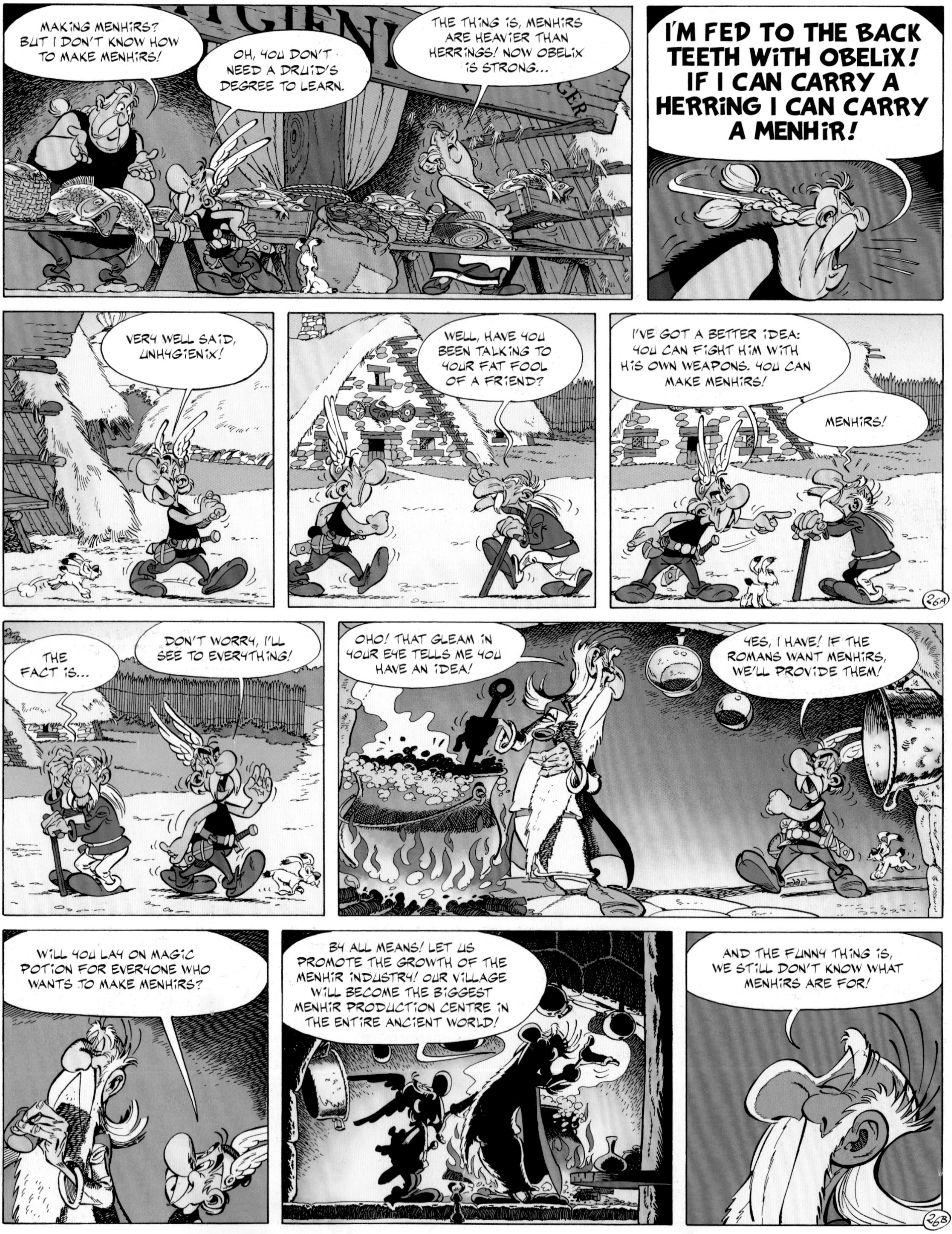
MAKING MENHIRS? BUT I DON'T KNOW HOW TO MAKE MENHIRS!
OH, YOU DON'T NEED A DRUID'S DEGREE TO LEARN.
THE THING IS, MENHIRS ARE HEAVIER THAN HERRINGS! NOW OBELIX IS STRONG...
I'M FED TO THE BACK TEETH WITH OBELIX! IF I CAN CARRY A HERRING I CAN CARRY A MENHIR!
VERY WELL SAID, UNHYGIENIX!
WELL, HAVE YOU BEEN TALKING TO YOUR FAT FOOL OF A FRIEND?
I'VE GOT A BETTER IDEA: YOU CAN FIGHT HIM WITH HIS OWN WEAPONS. YOU CAN MAKE MENHIRS!
MENHIRS!
26A
THE FACT IS...
DON'T WORRY, I'LL SEE TO EVERYTHING!
OHO! THAT GLEAM IN YOUR EYE TELLS ME YOU HAVE AN IDEA!
YES, I HAVE! IF THE ROMANS WANT MENHIRS, WE'LL PROVIDE THEM!
WILL YOU LAY ON MAGIC POTION FOR EVERYONE WHO WANTS TO MAKE MENHIRS?
BY ALL MEANS! LET US PROMOTE THE GROWTH OF THE MENHIR INDUSTRY! OUR VILLAGE WILL BECOME THE BIGGEST MENHIR PRODUCTION CENTRE IN THE ENTIRE ANCIENT WORLD!
AND THE FUNNY THING IS, WE STILL DON'T KNOW WHAT MENHIRS ARE FOR!
26B

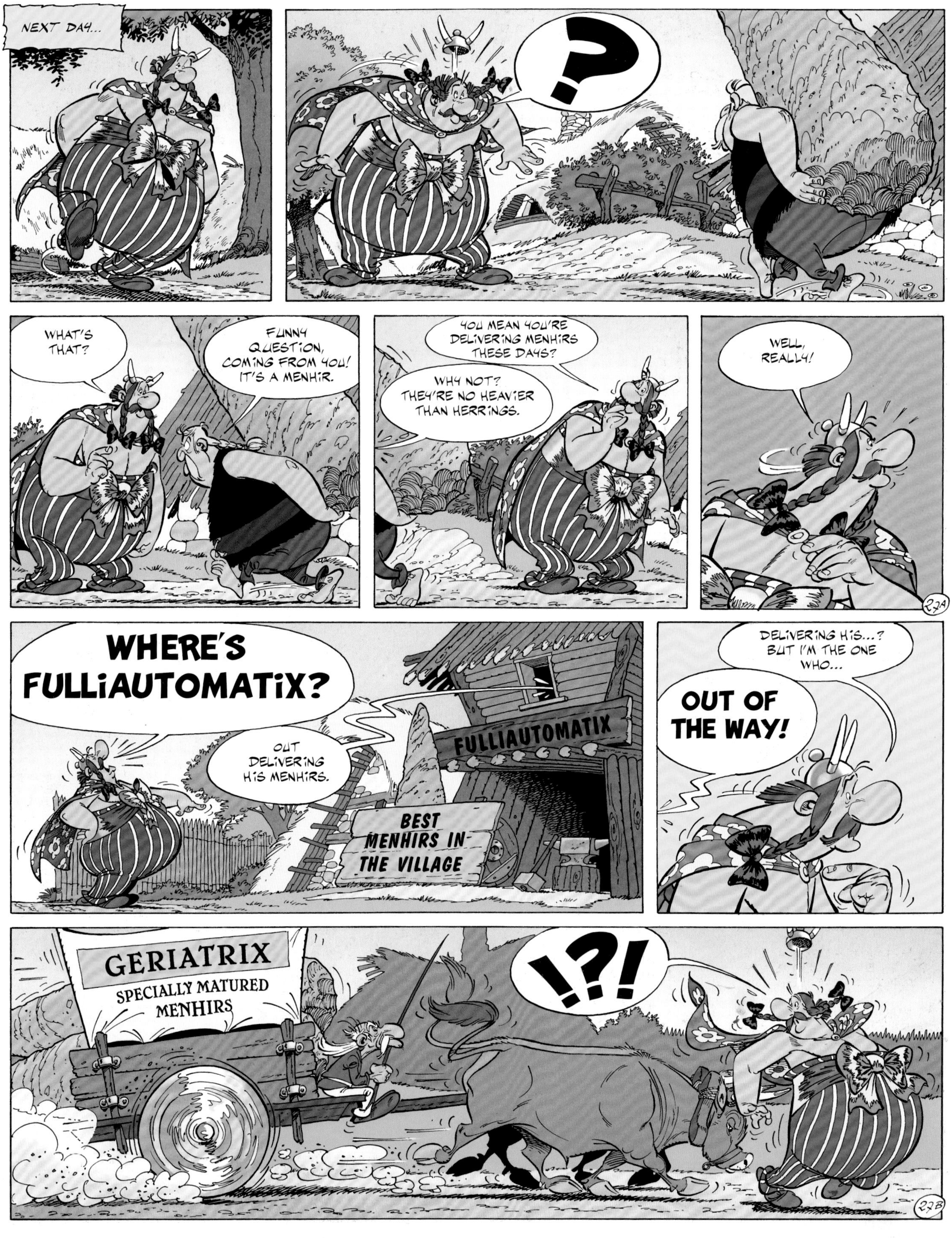

NEXT DAY...
?
WHAT'S THAT?
FUNNY QUESTION, COMING FROM YOU! IT'S A MENHIR.
YOU MEAN YOU'RE DELIVERING MENHIRS THESE DAYS?
WHY NOT? THEY'RE NO HEAVIER THAN HERRINGS.
WELL, REALLY!
27A
WHERE'S FULLIAUTOMATIX?
OUT DELIVERING HIS MENHIRS.
FULLIAUTOMATIX
BEST MENHIRS IN THE VILLAGE
DELIVERING HIS...? BUT I'M THE ONE WHO...
OUT OF THE WAY!
GERIATRIX
SPECIALLY MATURED MENHIRS
!?!
27B

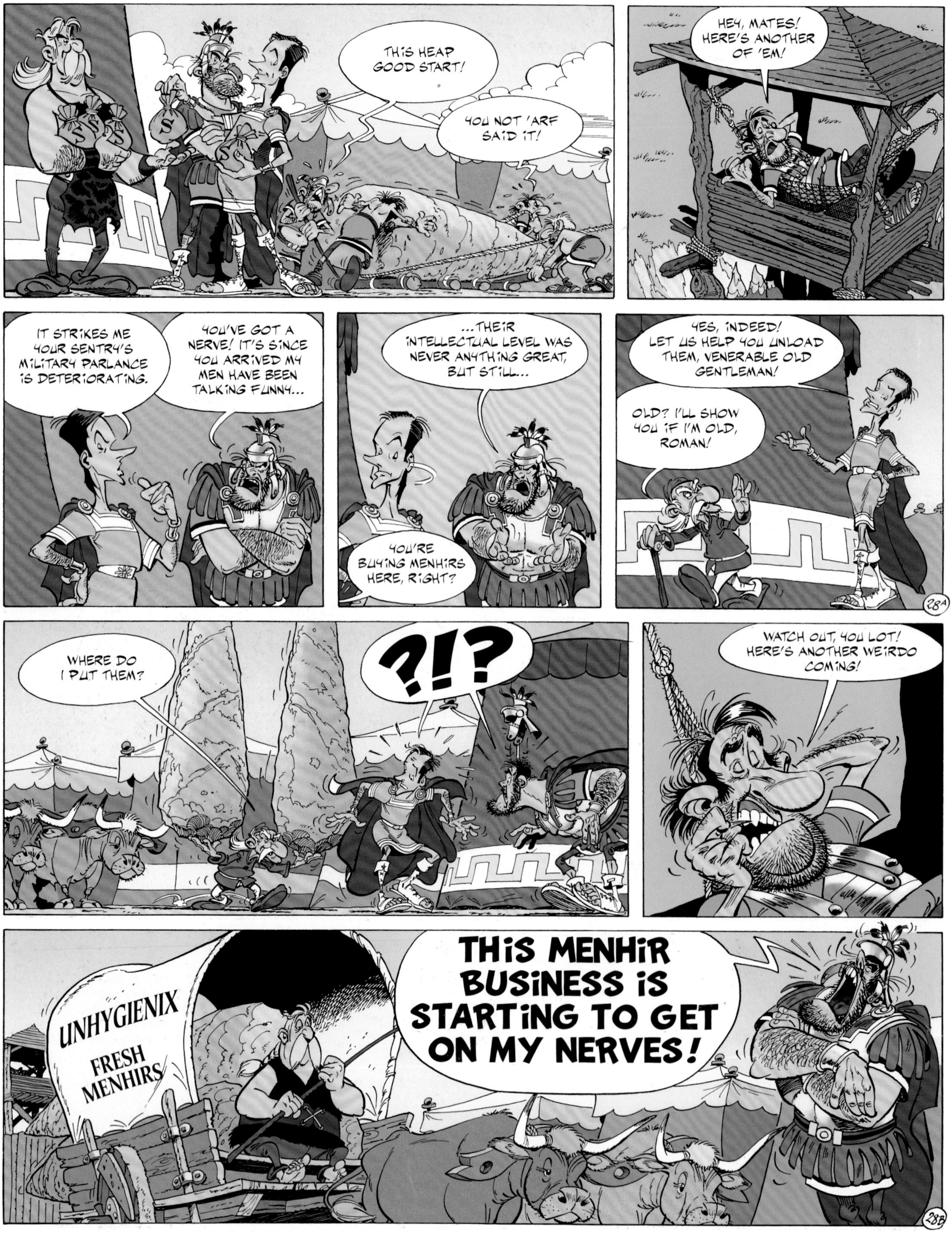
THIS HEAP GOOD START!
YOU NOT 'ARF SAID IT!
HEY, MATES! HERE'S ANOTHER OF 'EM!
IT STRIKES ME YOUR SENTRY'S MILITARY PARLANCE IS DETERIORATING.
YOU'VE GOT A NERVE! IT'S SINCE YOU ARRIVED MY MEN HAVE BEEN TALKING FUNNY...
...THEIR INTELLECTUAL LEVEL WAS NEVER ANYTHING GREAT, BUT STILL...
YOU'RE BUYING MENHIRS HERE, RIGHT?
YES, INDEED! LET US HELP YOU UNLOAD THEM, VENERABLE OLD GENTLEMAN!
OLD? I'LL SHOW YOU IF I'M OLD, ROMAN!
28A
WHERE DO I PUT THEM?
?!?
WATCH OUT, YOU LOT! HERE'S ANOTHER WEIRDO COMING!
UNHYGIENIX
FRESH MENHIRS
THIS MENHIR BUSINESS IS STARTING TO GET ON MY NERVES!
28B

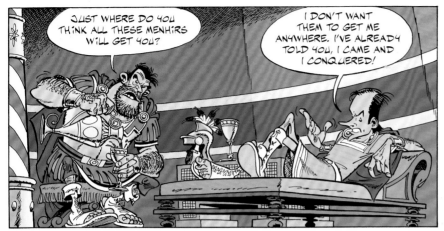

JUST WHERE DO YOU THINK ALL THESE MENHIRS WILL GET YOU?

I DON'T WANT THEM TO GET ME ANYWHERE. I'VE ALREADY TOLD YOU, I CAME AND I CONQUERED!

THE GAULS ARE ALL USING THEIR MAGIC POWERS TO MAKE MENHIRS, INSTEAD OF THUMPING OUR LEGIONARIES...

THEY HAVE BEEN DEFEATED BY THE PROFIT MOTIVE! GOLD AND HIGH LIVING WILL WEAKEN THEIR MORAL FIBRE. DON'T YOU AGREE?

WELL... MAYBE...

WHAT ARE WE GOING TO DO WITH THIS BIG HEAP OF MENHIRS?

BUT TAKE A LOOK AT THIS!

REDDE CAESARI QUAE SUNT CAESARIS.

UH?

RENDER UNTO CAESAR HEAP BIG HEAP MENHIRS THAT ARE CAESAR'S.

DON'T SPEAK TO ME LIKE THAT! YOUR MENHIRS ARE CAUSING SOFTENING OF THE BRAIN ALL ROUND!

CAESAR HAS PAID FOR THESE MENHIRS, SO IT'S ONLY RIGHT FOR ME TO DELIVER THEM. WHILE I'M AWAY, CARRY ON BUYING MENHIRS, AND KEEP RAISING THE PRICE. SI VIS PACEM, BUY MENHIRS!

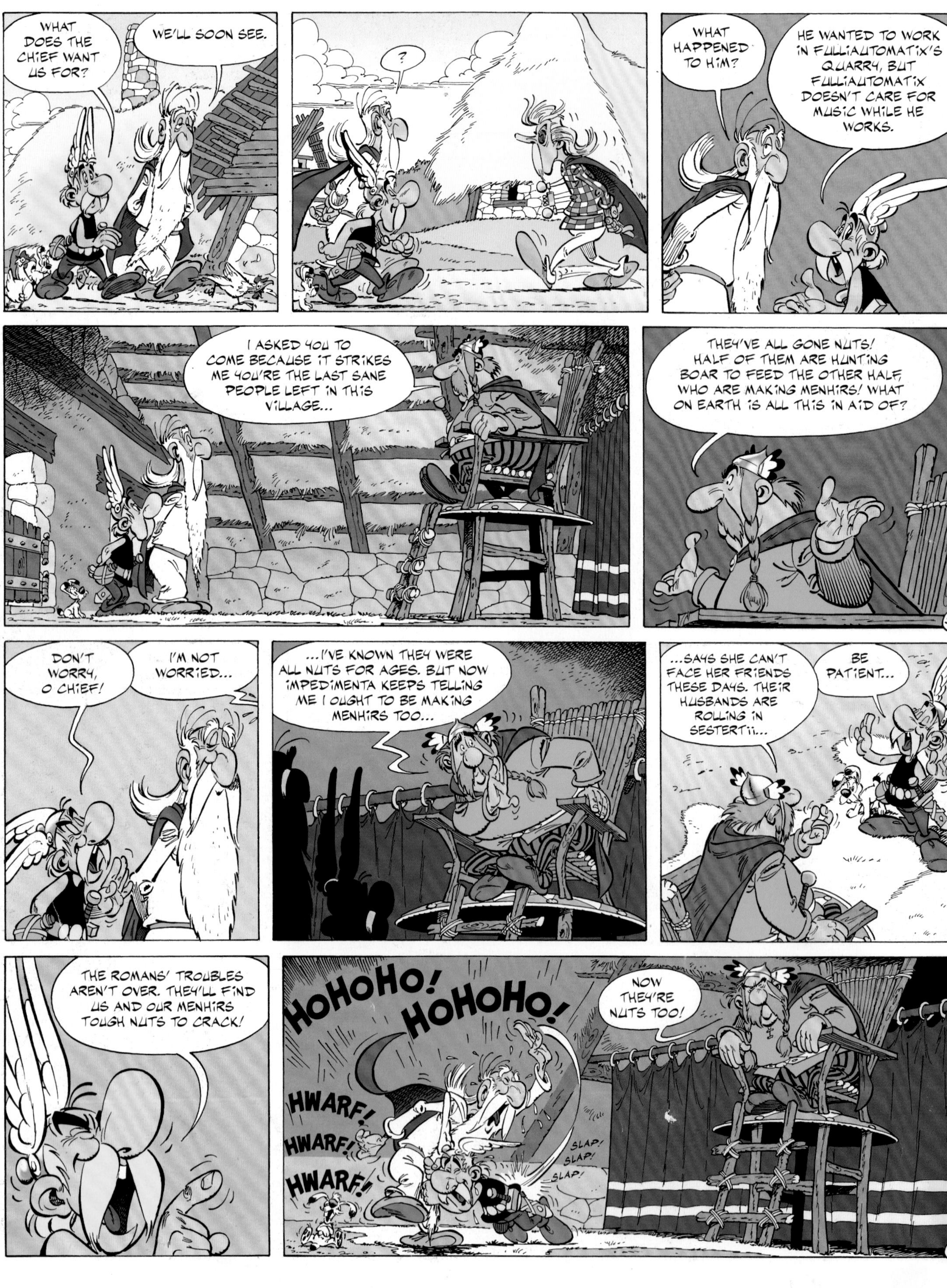
WHAT DOES THE CHIEF WANT US FOR?
WE'LL SOON SEE.
?
WHAT HAPPENED TO HIM?
HE WANTED TO WORK IN FULLIAUTOMATIX'S QUARRY, BUT FULLIAUTOMATIX DOESN'T CARE FOR MUSIC WHILE HE WORKS.
I ASKED YOU TO COME BECAUSE IT STRIKES ME YOU'RE THE LAST SANE PEOPLE LEFT IN THIS VILLAGE...
THEY'VE ALL GONE NUTS! HALF OF THEM ARE HUNTING BOAR TO FEED THE OTHER HALF, WHO ARE MAKING MENHIRS! WHAT ON EARTH IS ALL THIS IN AID OF?
DON'T WORRY, O CHIEF!
I'M NOT WORRIED...
...I'VE KNOWN THEY WERE ALL NUTS FOR AGES. BUT NOW IMPEDIMENTA KEEPS TELLING ME I OUGHT TO BE MAKING MENHIRS TOO...
...SAYS SHE CAN'T FACE HER FRIENDS THESE DAYS. THEIR HUSBANDS ARE ROLLING IN SESTERTII...
BE PATIENT...
THE ROMANS' TROUBLES AREN'T OVER. THEY'LL FIND US AND OUR MENHIRS TOUGH NUTS TO CRACK!
HOHOHO! HOHOHO!
HWARF! HWARF! HWARF!
SLAP! SLAP! SLAP!
NOW THEY'RE NUTS TOO!

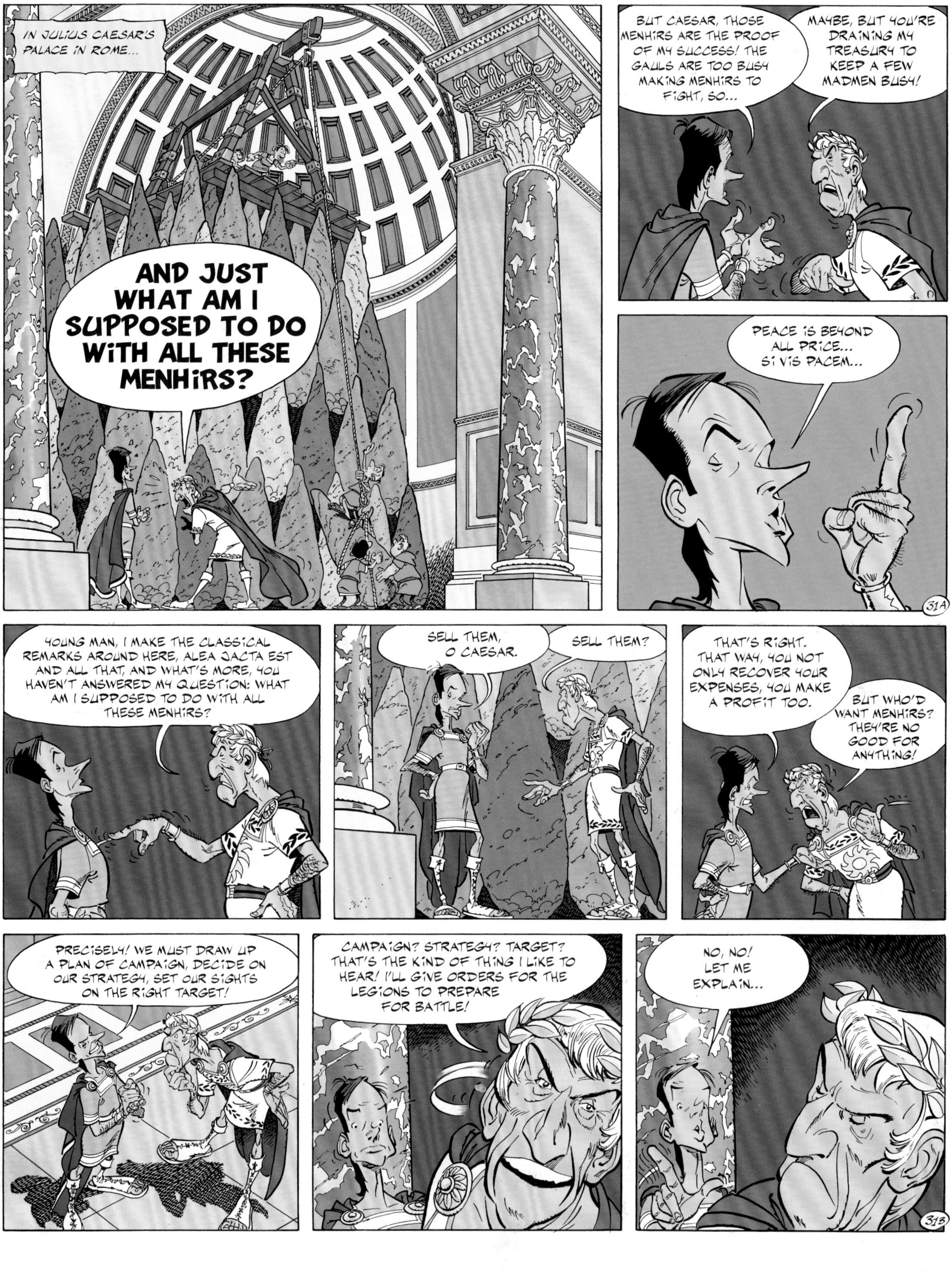
IN JULIUS CAESAR'S PALACE IN ROME...
AND JUST WHAT AM I SUPPOSED TO DO WITH ALL THESE MENHIRS?
BUT CAESAR, THOSE MENHIRS ARE THE PROOF OF MY SUCCESS! THE GAULS ARE TOO BUSY MAKING MENHIRS TO FIGHT, SO...
MAYBE, BUT YOU'RE DRAINING MY TREASURY TO KEEP A FEW MADMEN BUSY!
PEACE IS BEYOND ALL PRICE... SI VIS PACEM...
31A
YOUNG MAN, I MAKE THE CLASSICAL REMARKS AROUND HERE, ALEA JACTA EST AND ALL THAT, AND WHAT'S MORE, YOU HAVEN'T ANSWERED MY QUESTION: WHAT AM I SUPPOSED TO DO WITH ALL THESE MENHIRS?
SELL THEM, O CAESAR.
SELL THEM?
THAT'S RIGHT. THAT WAY, YOU NOT ONLY RECOVER YOUR EXPENSES, YOU MAKE A PROFIT TOO.
BUT WHO'D WANT MENHIRS? THEY'RE NO GOOD FOR ANYTHING!
PRECISELY! WE MUST DRAW UP A PLAN OF CAMPAIGN, DECIDE ON OUR STRATEGY, SET OUR SIGHTS ON THE RIGHT TARGET!
CAMPAIGN? STRATEGY? TARGET? THAT'S THE KIND OF THING I LIKE TO HEAR! I'LL GIVE ORDERS FOR THE LEGIONS TO PREPARE FOR BATTLE!
NO, NO! LET ME EXPLAIN...
31B

THE FOLLOWING PASSAGE WILL BE DIFFICULT FOR THOSE OF YOU UNACQUAINTED WITH THE ANCIENT BUSINESS WORLD TO UNDERSTAND, ESPECIALLY AS, THESE DAYS, SUCH A STATE OF AFFAIRS COULD NEVER EXIST, SINCE NO ONE WOULD DREAM OF TRYING TO SELL SOMETHING UTTERLY USELESS...
AT THIS PRESENT MOMENT IN TIME THE DEMAND FOR MENHIRS IS VIRTUALLY NIL. THEREFORE WE MUST BE CREATIVE... FIND HOW TO APPEAL TO THE POTENTIAL CONSUMER...
I
A B C D
LET US STUDY THOSE FACTORS WHICH WILL ALLOW US TO HOME IN ON OUR TARGET...
PEOPLE WILL BUY: A: SOMETHING USEFUL; B: SOMETHING COMFORTABLE; C: SOMETHING THAT'S FUN; D: SOMETHING TO MAKE THE NEIGHBOURS ENVIOUS. WE HAVE TO AIM FOR D!
A CAMPAIGN CENTRED ON A CAREFULLY DEFINED AREA SHOULD ALLOW US TO MAKE RAPID CONTACT WITH A LARGE BODY OF CONSUMERS ABLE TO ABSORB OUR STOCKS AT MAXIMUM SPEED...
32A
II
INSTANT RECOGNITION OF THE PRODUCT WILL BE OBTAINED BY INTENSIVE REPETITION OF THE QUALITIES OF THE AFORESAID PRODUCT...
III
A B C
...WHICH MAY BE DEFINED AS FOLLOWS: A: DURABILITY; B: SOLIDITY; C: OTHER QUALITIES.
IV
DEC. NOV. OCT. SEPT. SEX. QVIN. JVN. MAI. APR. MARS. FEB. JAN.
THUS I MAKE NO RASH PROMISES WHEN I SAY THAT WE SHOULD SUCCEED IN OBTAINING POSITIVE RESULTS, SALESWISE, AT NO VERY DISTANT DATE.
UH?
ME THINK YOU ABLE SELL HEAP BIG HEAP MENHIRS PLENTY QUICK.
UDERZO & GOSCINNY
ALBO NOTAMBA LAPILLO
32B

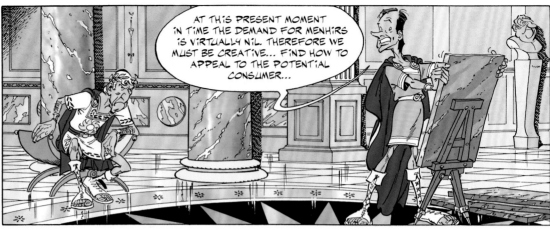

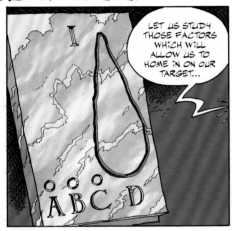

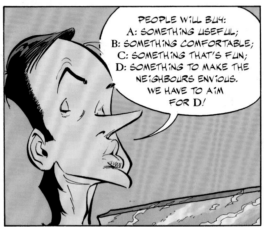

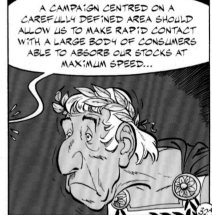

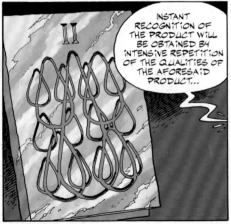

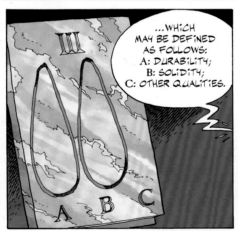

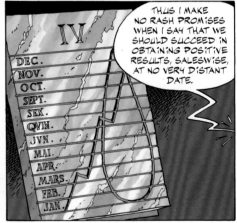

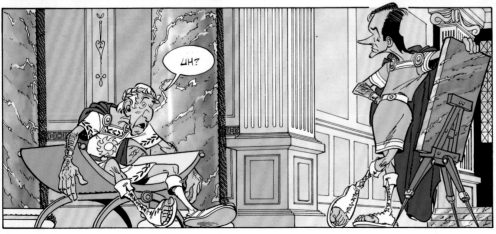

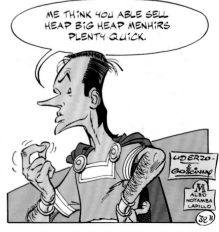

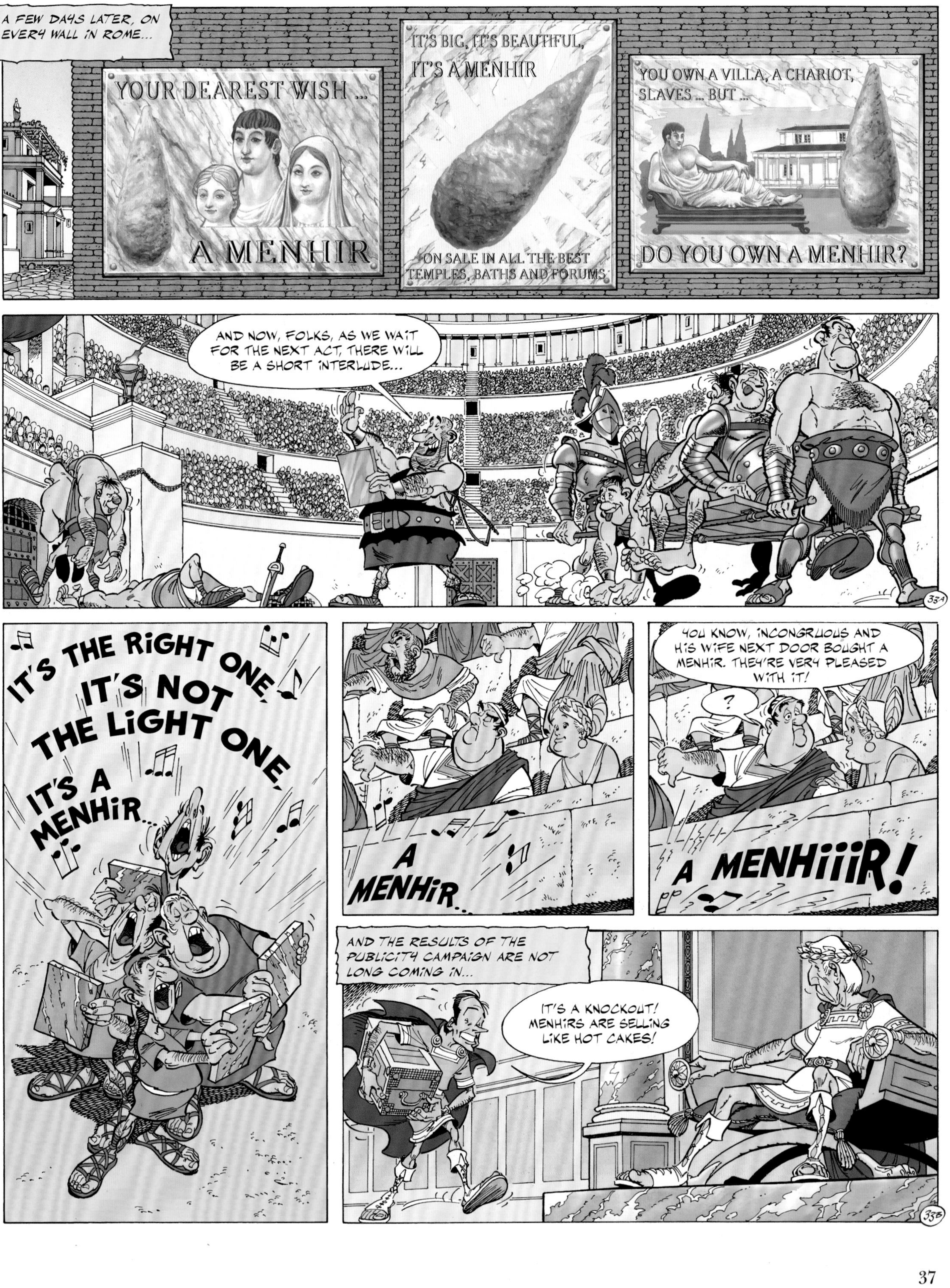
A FEW DAYS LATER, ON EVERY WALL IN ROME...
YOUR DEAREST WISH ...
A MENHIR
IT'S BIG, IT'S BEAUTIFUL,
IT'S A MENHIR
ON SALE IN ALL THE BEST TEMPLES, BATHS AND FORUMS
YOU OWN A VILLA, A CHARIOT, SLAVES ... BUT ...
DO YOU OWN A MENHIR?
AND NOW, FOLKS, AS WE WAIT FOR THE NEXT ACT, THERE WILL BE A SHORT INTERLUDE...
IT'S THE RIGHT ONE, IT'S NOT THE LIGHT ONE, IT'S A MENHIR...
A MENHIR...
YOU KNOW, INCONGRUOUS AND HIS WIFE NEXT DOOR BOUGHT A MENHIR. THEY'RE VERY PLEASED WITH IT!
?
A MENHIIIR!
AND THE RESULTS OF THE PUBLICITY CAMPAIGN ARE NOT LONG COMING IN...
IT'S A KNOCKOUT! MENHIRS ARE SELLING LIKE HOT CAKES!

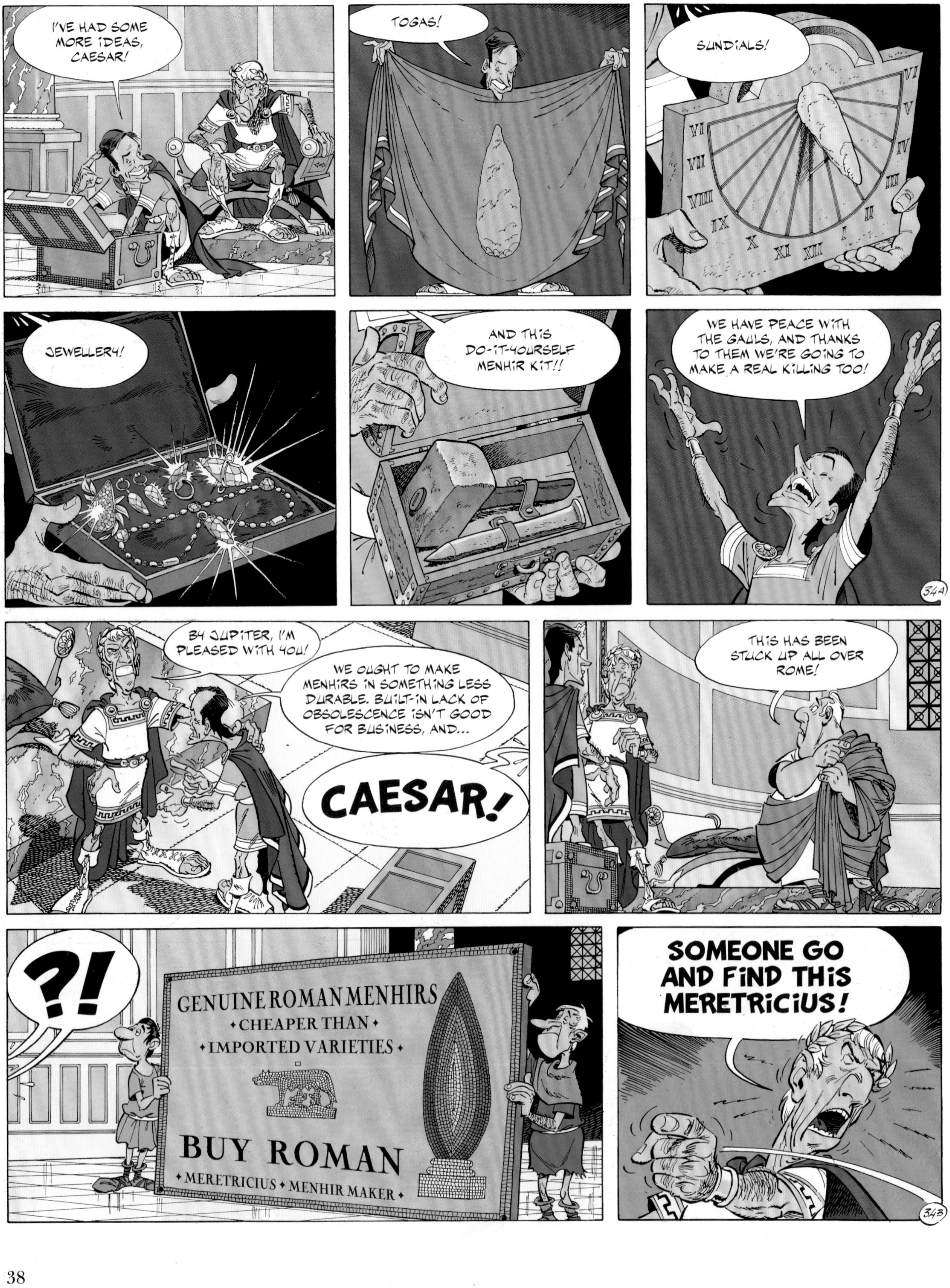
I'VE HAD SOME MORE IDEAS, CAESAR!
TOGAS!
SUNDIALS!
VI V IV III II I XII XI X IX VIII VII VI
JEWELLERY!
AND THIS DO-IT-YOURSELF MENHIR KIT!!
WE HAVE PEACE WITH THE GAULS, AND THANKS TO THEM WE'RE GOING TO MAKE A REAL KILLING TOO!
34A
BY JUPITER, I'M PLEASED WITH YOU!
WE OUGHT TO MAKE MENHIRS IN SOMETHING LESS DURABLE. BUILT-IN LACK OF OBSOLESCENCE ISN'T GOOD FOR BUSINESS, AND...
CAESAR!
THIS HAS BEEN STUCK UP ALL OVER ROME!
?!
GENUINE ROMAN MENHIRS
• CHEAPER THAN •
• IMPORTED VARIETIES •
BUY ROMAN
• MERETRICIUS • MENHIR MAKER •
SOMEONE GO AND FIND THIS MERETRICIUS!
34B

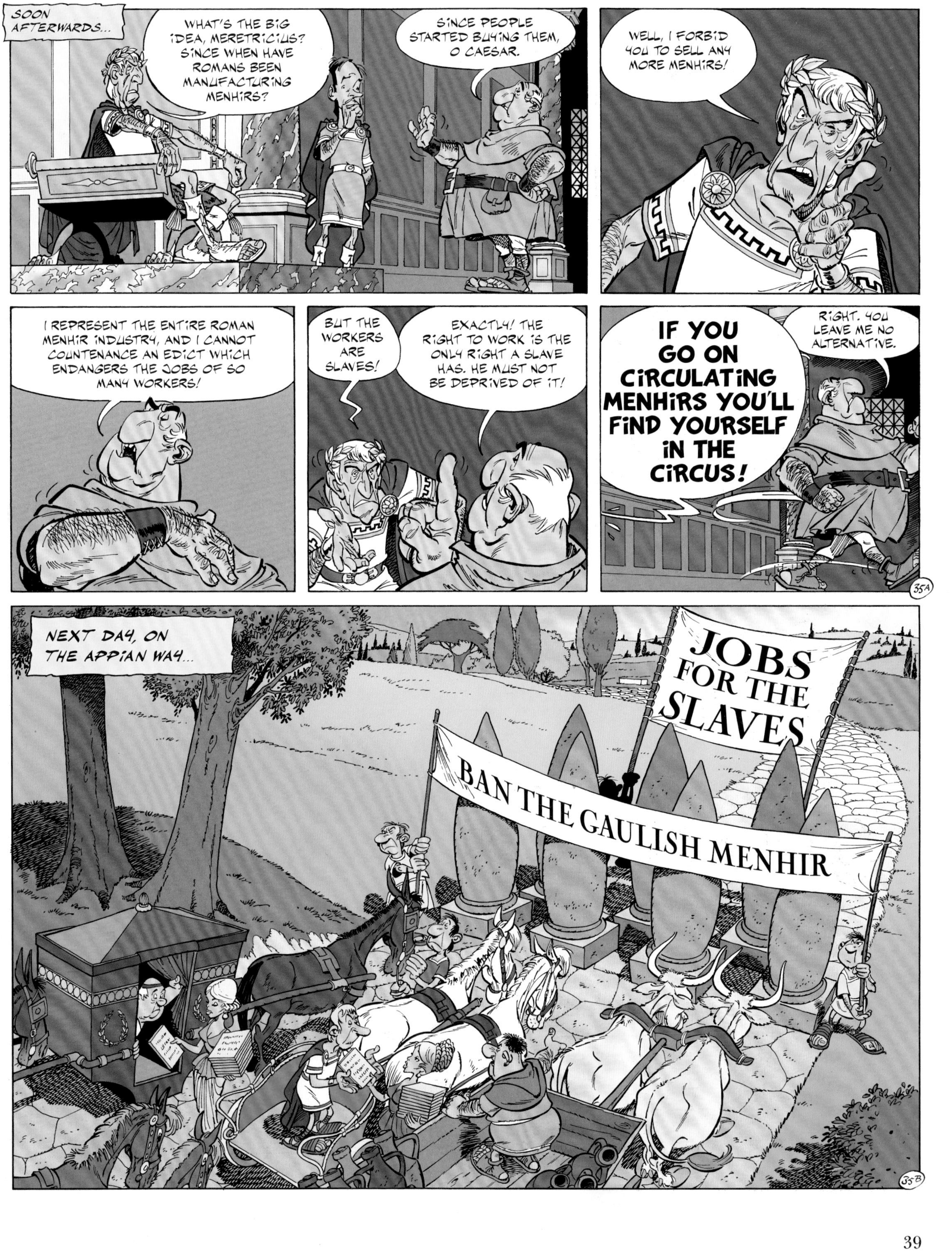
SOON AFTERWARDS...
WHAT'S THE BIG IDEA, MERETRICIUS? SINCE WHEN HAVE ROMANS BEEN MANUFACTURING MENHIRS?
SINCE PEOPLE STARTED BUYING THEM, O CAESAR.
WELL, I FORBID YOU TO SELL ANY MORE MENHIRS!
I REPRESENT THE ENTIRE ROMAN MENHIR INDUSTRY, AND I CANNOT COUNTENANCE AN EDICT WHICH ENDANGERS THE JOBS OF SO MANY WORKERS!
BUT THE WORKERS ARE SLAVES!
EXACTLY! THE RIGHT TO WORK IS THE ONLY RIGHT A SLAVE HAS. HE MUST NOT BE DEPRIVED OF IT!
IF YOU GO ON CIRCULATING MENHIRS YOU'LL FIND YOURSELF IN THE CIRCUS!
RIGHT. YOU LEAVE ME NO ALTERNATIVE.
NEXT DAY, ON THE APPIAN WAY...
JOBS FOR THE SLAVES
BAN THE GAULISH MENHIR

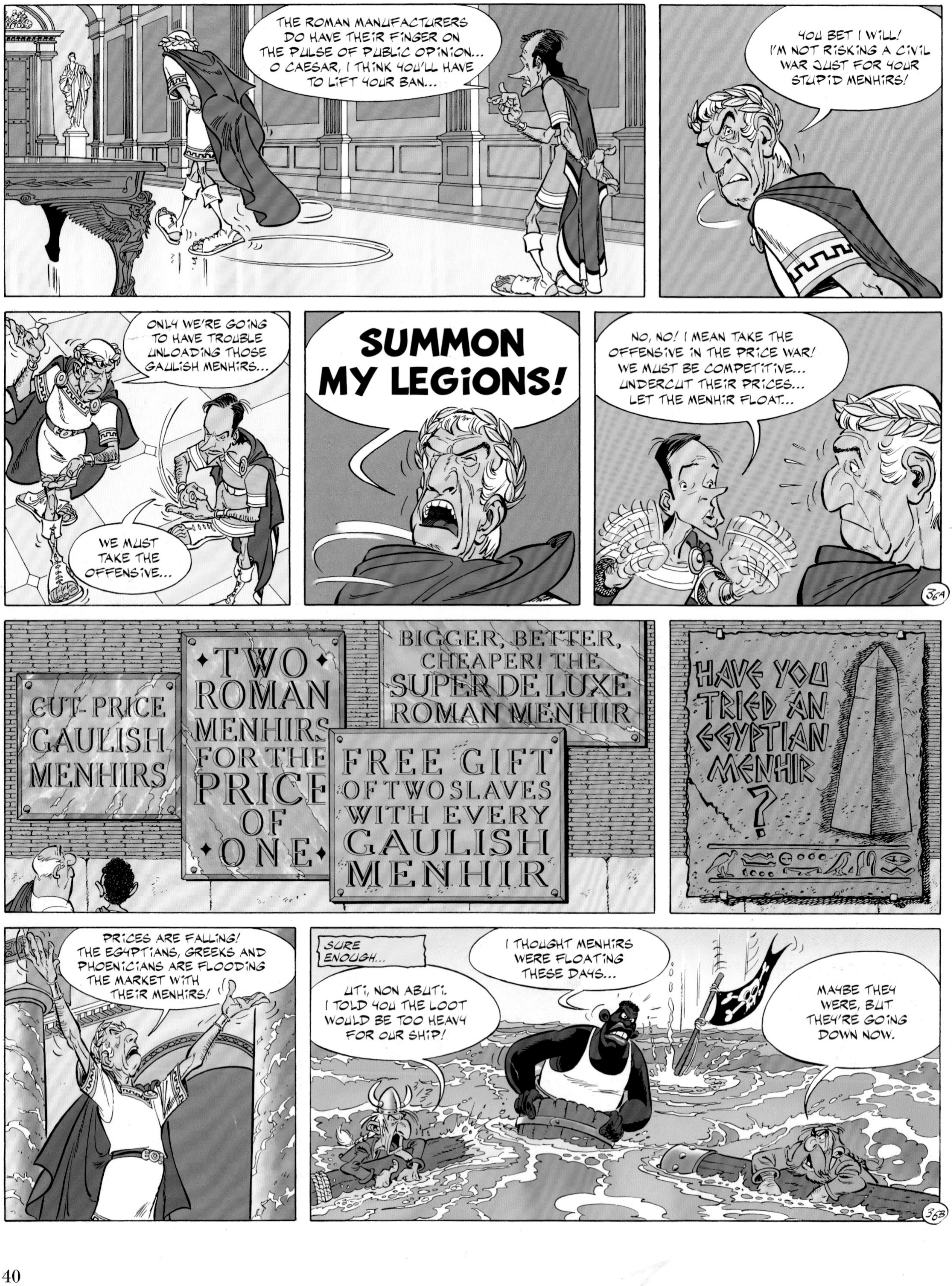
THE ROMAN MANUFACTURERS DO HAVE THEIR FINGER ON THE PULSE OF PUBLIC OPINION... O CAESAR, I THINK YOU'LL HAVE TO LIFT YOUR BAN...
YOU BET I WILL! I'M NOT RISKING A CIVIL WAR JUST FOR YOUR STUPID MENHIRS!
ONLY WE'RE GOING TO HAVE TROUBLE UNLOADING THOSE GAULISH MENHIRS...
WE MUST TAKE THE OFFENSIVE...
SUMMON MY LEGIONS!
NO, NO! I MEAN TAKE THE OFFENSIVE IN THE PRICE WAR! WE MUST BE COMPETITIVE... UNDERCUT THEIR PRICES... LET THE MENHIR FLOAT...
CUT-PRICE GAULISH MENHIRS
TWO ROMAN MENHIRS FOR THE PRICE OF ONE
BIGGER, BETTER, CHEAPER! THE SUPER DE LUXE ROMAN MENHIR
FREE GIFT OF TWO SLAVES WITH EVERY GAULISH MENHIR
HAVE YOU TRIED AN EGYPTIAN MENHIR ?
PRICES ARE FALLING! THE EGYPTIANS, GREEKS AND PHOENICIANS ARE FLOODING THE MARKET WITH THEIR MENHIRS!
SURE ENOUGH...
I THOUGHT MENHIRS WERE FLOATING THESE DAYS...
UTI, NON ABUTI. I TOLD YOU THE LOOT WOULD BE TOO HEAVY FOR OUR SHIP!
MAYBE THEY WERE, BUT THEY'RE GOING DOWN NOW.

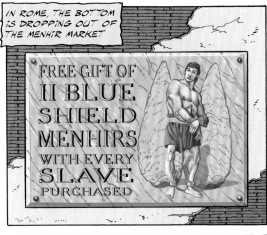

IN ROME, THE BOTTOM IS DROPPING OUT OF THE MENHIR MARKET

FREE GIFT OF II BLUE SHIELD MENHIRS WITH EVERY SLAVE PURCHASED

PEOPLE DON'T EVEN WANT THEM AS A GIFT... WELL, THAT'S TOO BAD! I'VE LOST A FORTUNE, BUT LET'S FORGET IT...

THE THING IS...

YES?

WELL, IT'S LIKE THIS, O CAESAR...

I WANTED TO KEEP THE PEACE IN GAUL, SO BEFORE I LEFT I GAVE ORDERS FOR THEM TO GO ON BUYING MENHIRS... AND RAISING THE PRICE.

WHAT? YOU KNOW THE STATE OF MY FINANCES? AND YOU SAID WE'D MAKE A KILLING! GET BACK TO GAUL AND STOP IT!!!

ER... YOU WOULDN'T LIKE TO SEND SOMEONE ELSE, WOULD YOU? I HAVE A FRIEND WHO WAS AT BUSINESS SCHOOL WITH ME. HE...

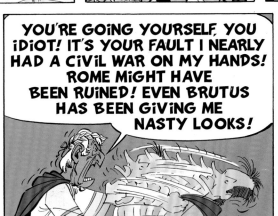

YOU'RE GOING YOURSELF, YOU IDIOT! IT'S YOUR FAULT I NEARLY HAD A CIVIL WAR ON MY HANDS! ROME MIGHT HAVE BEEN RUINED! EVEN BRUTUS HAS BEEN GIVING ME NASTY LOOKS!

BUT... BUT THEY'LL KILL ME!

THAT PARTICULAR KILLING WOULDN'T WORRY ME!

ANYWAY, IF YOU DON'T GO I'LL HAVE YOU THROWN TO THE LIONS!!

MENHIR GRAVEYARD

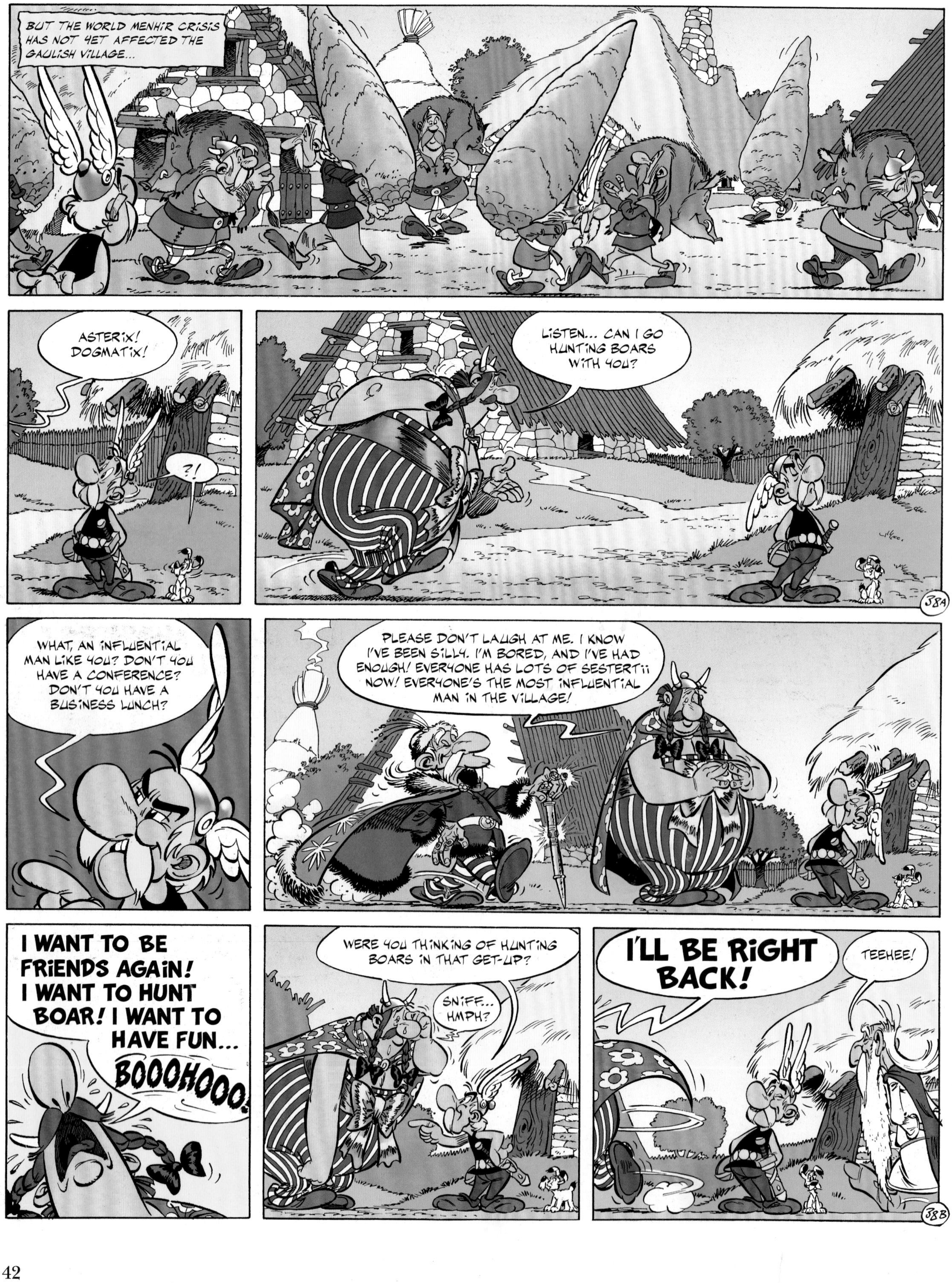

BUT THE WORLD MENHIR CRISIS HAS NOT YET AFFECTED THE GAULISH VILLAGE...
ASTERIX! DOGMATIX!
?!
LISTEN... CAN I GO HUNTING BOARS WITH YOU?
38A
WHAT, AN INFLUENTIAL MAN LIKE YOU? DON'T YOU HAVE A CONFERENCE? DON'T YOU HAVE A BUSINESS LUNCH?
PLEASE DON'T LAUGH AT ME. I KNOW I'VE BEEN SILLY. I'M BORED, AND I'VE HAD ENOUGH! EVERYONE HAS LOTS OF SESTERTII NOW! EVERYONE'S THE MOST INFLUENTIAL MAN IN THE VILLAGE!
I WANT TO BE FRIENDS AGAIN! I WANT TO HUNT BOAR! I WANT TO HAVE FUN...
BOOOHOOO!
WERE YOU THINKING OF HUNTING BOARS IN THAT GET-UP?
SNIFF... HMPH?
I'LL BE RIGHT BACK!
TEEHEE!
38B

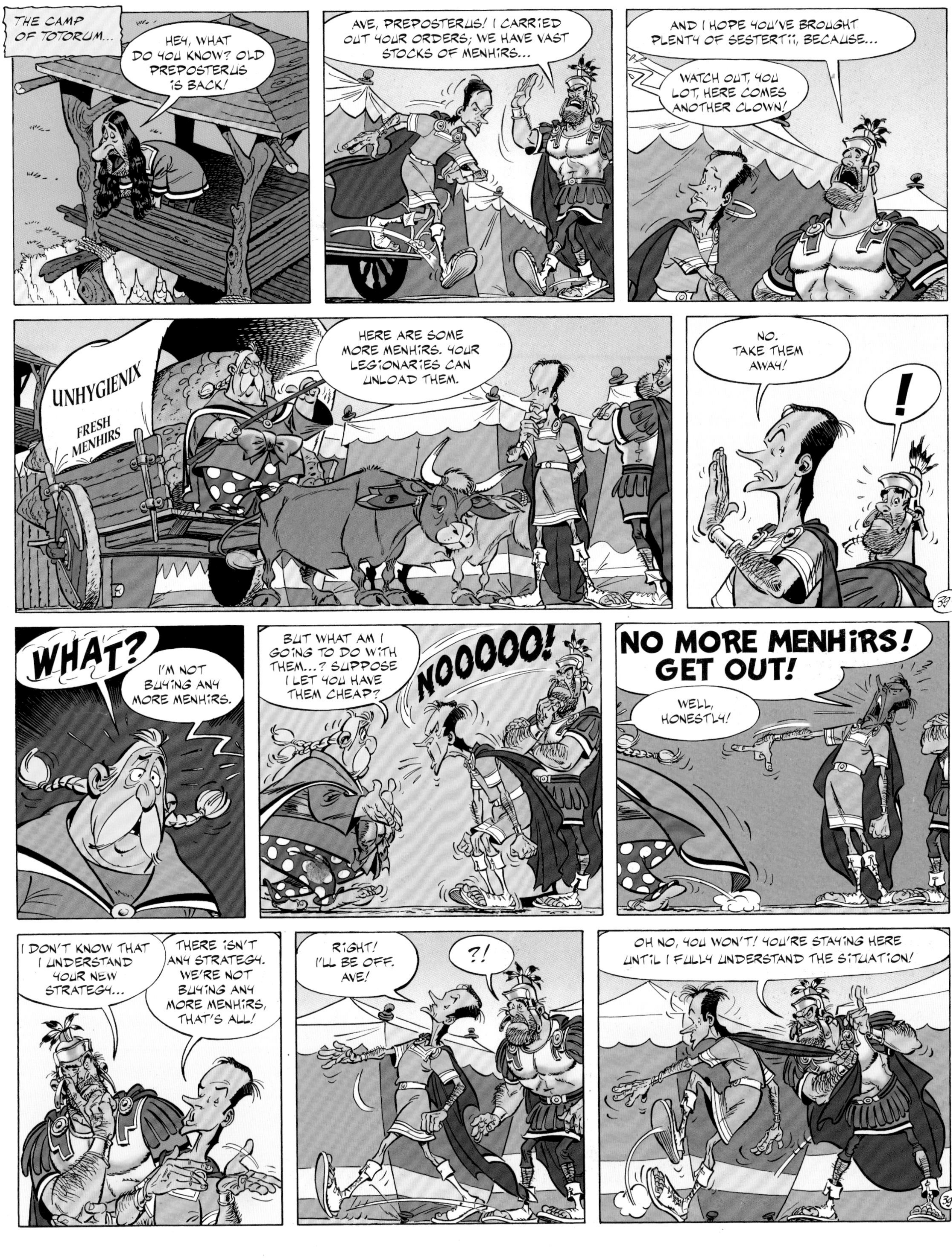

THE CAMP OF TOTORUM...
HEY, WHAT DO YOU KNOW? OLD PREPOSTERUS IS BACK!
AVE, PREPOSTERUS! I CARRIED OUT YOUR ORDERS; WE HAVE VAST STOCKS OF MENHIRS...
AND I HOPE YOU'VE BROUGHT PLENTY OF SESTERTII, BECAUSE...
WATCH OUT, YOU LOT, HERE COMES ANOTHER CLOWN!
UNHYGIENIX
FRESH MENHIRS
HERE ARE SOME MORE MENHIRS. YOUR LEGIONARIES CAN UNLOAD THEM.
NO. TAKE THEM AWAY!
!
WHAT?
I'M NOT BUYING ANY MORE MENHIRS.
BUT WHAT AM I GOING TO DO WITH THEM...? SUPPOSE I LET YOU HAVE THEM CHEAP?
NOOOOO!
NO MORE MENHIRS! GET OUT!
WELL, HONESTLY!
I DON'T KNOW THAT I UNDERSTAND YOUR NEW STRATEGY...
THERE ISN'T ANY STRATEGY. WE'RE NOT BUYING ANY MORE MENHIRS, THAT'S ALL!
RIGHT! I'LL BE OFF. AVE!
?!
OH NO, YOU WON'T! YOU'RE STAYING HERE UNTIL I FULLY UNDERSTAND THE SITUATION!

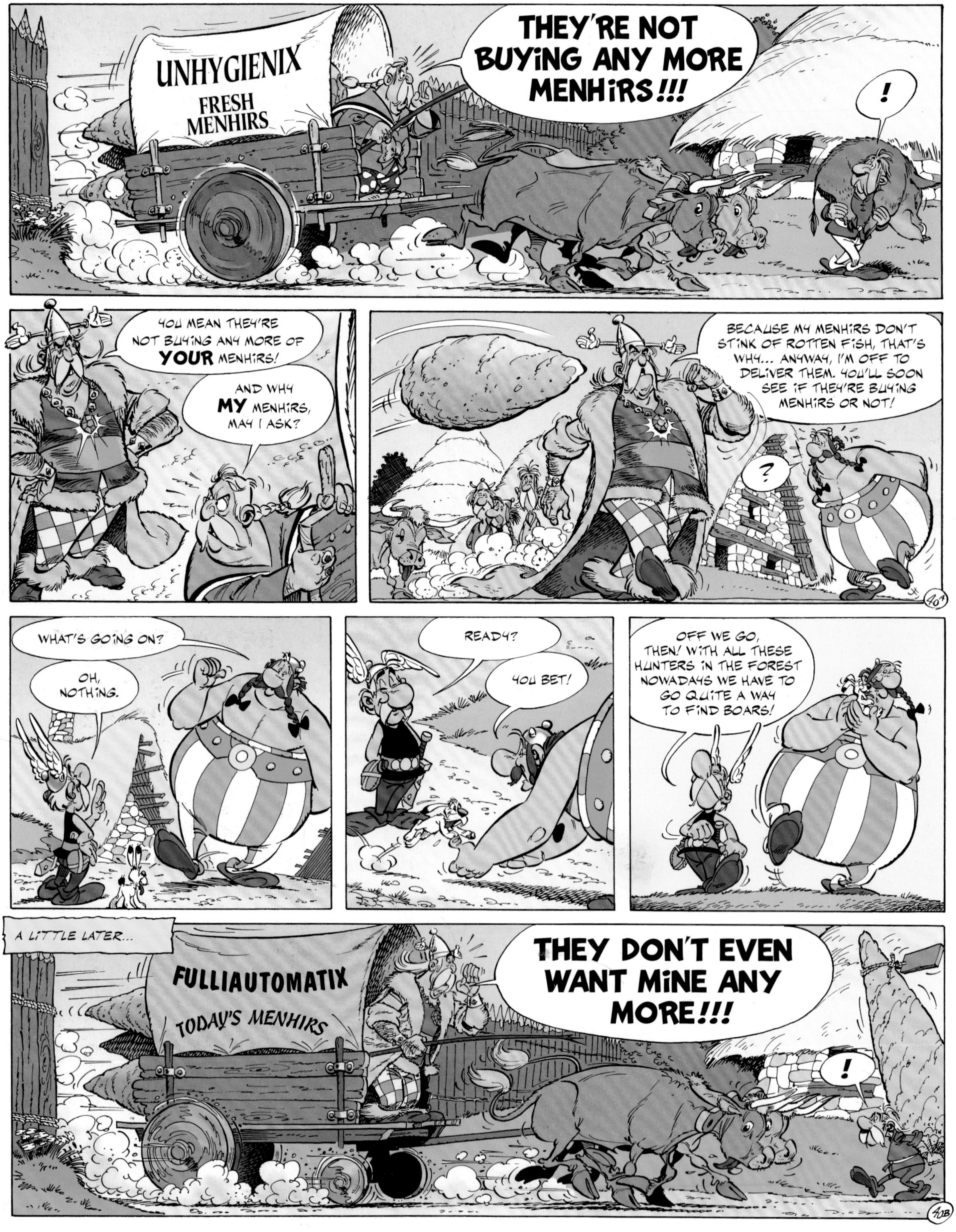
UNHYGIENIX
FRESH MENHIRS
THEY'RE NOT BUYING ANY MORE MENHIRS!!!
!
YOU MEAN THEY'RE NOT BUYING ANY MORE OF YOUR MENHIRS!
AND WHY MY MENHIRS, MAY I ASK?
BECAUSE MY MENHIRS DON'T STINK OF ROTTEN FISH, THAT'S WHY... ANYWAY, I'M OFF TO DELIVER THEM. YOU'LL SOON SEE IF THEY'RE BUYING MENHIRS OR NOT!
?
WHAT'S GOING ON?
OH, NOTHING.
READY?
YOU BET!
OFF WE GO, THEN! WITH ALL THESE HUNTERS IN THE FOREST NOWADAYS WE HAVE TO GO QUITE A WAY TO FIND BOARS!
A LITTLE LATER...
FULLIAUTOMATIX
TODAY'S MENHIRS
THEY DON'T EVEN WANT MINE ANY MORE!!!
!

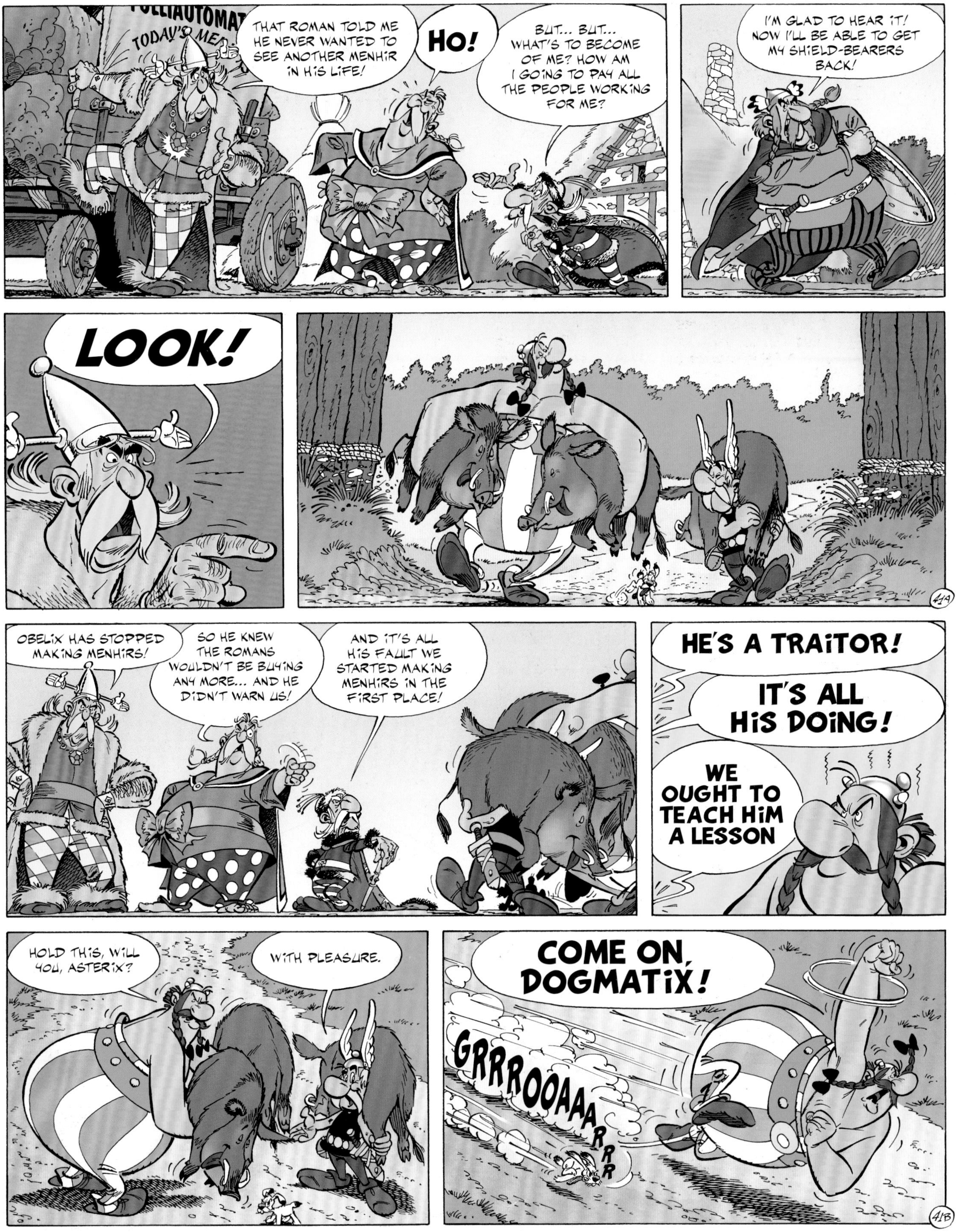

THAT ROMAN TOLD ME HE NEVER WANTED TO SEE ANOTHER MENHIR IN HIS LIFE!
HO!
BUT... BUT... WHAT'S TO BECOME OF ME? HOW AM I GOING TO PAY ALL THE PEOPLE WORKING FOR ME?
I'M GLAD TO HEAR IT! NOW I'LL BE ABLE TO GET MY SHIELD-BEARERS BACK!
LOOK!
OBELIX HAS STOPPED MAKING MENHIRS!
SO HE KNEW THE ROMANS WOULDN'T BE BUYING ANY MORE... AND HE DIDN'T WARN US!
AND IT'S ALL HIS FAULT WE STARTED MAKING MENHIRS IN THE FIRST PLACE!
HE'S A TRAITOR!
IT'S ALL HIS DOING!
WE OUGHT TO TEACH HIM A LESSON
HOLD THIS, WILL YOU, ASTERIX?
WITH PLEASURE.
COME ON, DOGMATIX!
GRRROOAAARRR

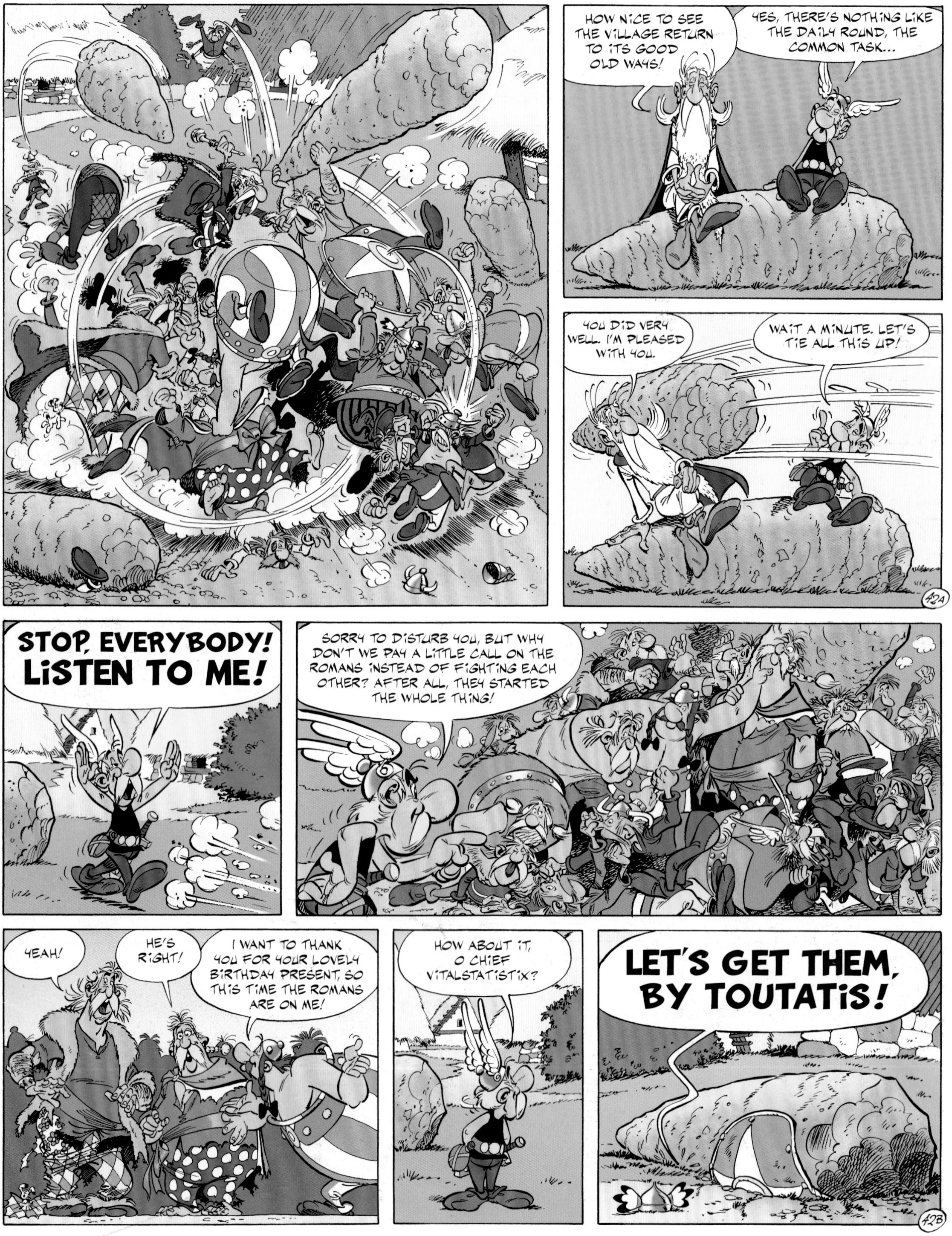
HOW NICE TO SEE THE VILLAGE RETURN TO ITS GOOD OLD WAYS!
YES, THERE'S NOTHING LIKE THE DAILY ROUND, THE COMMON TASK...
YOU DID VERY WELL. I'M PLEASED WITH YOU.
WAIT A MINUTE. LET'S TIE ALL THIS UP!
STOP, EVERYBODY! LISTEN TO ME!
SORRY TO DISTURB YOU, BUT WHY DON'T WE PAY A LITTLE CALL ON THE ROMANS INSTEAD OF FIGHTING EACH OTHER? AFTER ALL, THEY STARTED THE WHOLE THING!
YEAH!
HE'S RIGHT!
I WANT TO THANK YOU FOR YOUR LOVELY BIRTHDAY PRESENT, SO THIS TIME THE ROMANS ARE ON ME!
HOW ABOUT IT, O CHIEF VITALSTATISTIX?
LET'S GET THEM, BY TOUTATIS!

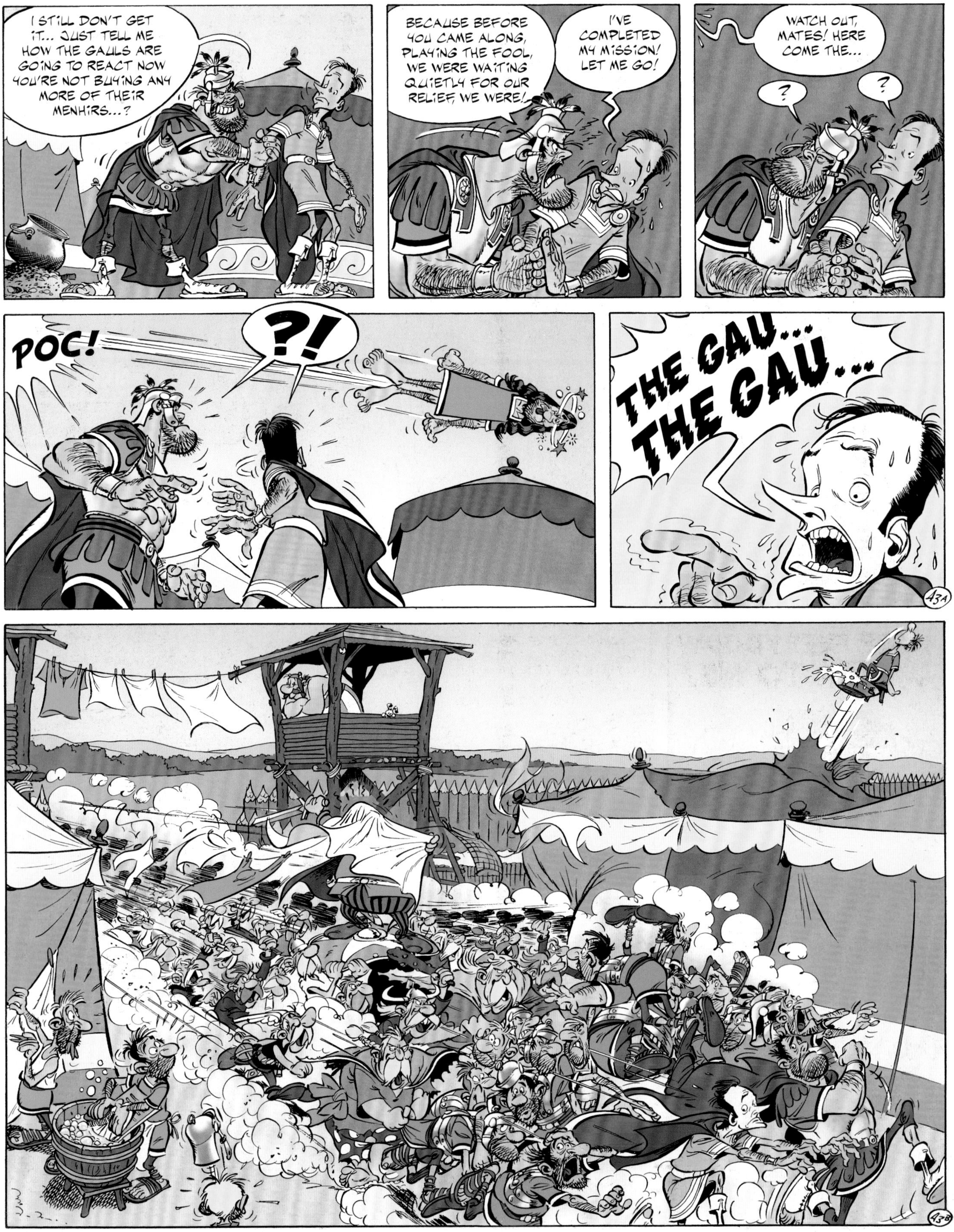
I STILL DON'T GET IT... JUST TELL ME HOW THE GAULS ARE GOING TO REACT NOW YOU'RE NOT BUYING ANY MORE OF THEIR MENHIRS...?
BECAUSE BEFORE YOU CAME ALONG, PLAYING THE FOOL, WE WERE WAITING QUIETLY FOR OUR RELIEF, WE WERE!
I'VE COMPLETED MY MISSION! LET ME GO!
WATCH OUT, MATES! HERE COME THE...
?
?
POC!
?!
THE GAU... THE GAU...

THEY'VE FINISHED THEIR ATTACKS! RELIEF HERE, IS IT?

DUNNO, BUT WE SHOULD BE DUE FOR A TAX RELIEF ALL RIGHT AFTER THIS...

HEAP BIG WHIZZ-KID, EH? YOU SAVVY?

ALL OUR FRIENDS ARE ROLLING IN SESTERTII... WHAT WILL THEY DO WITH THEM?

NOT MUCH...

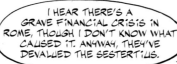

I HEAR THERE'S A GRAVE FINANCIAL CRISIS IN ROME, THOUGH I DON'T KNOW WHAT CAUSED IT. ANYWAY, THEY'VE DEVALUED THE SESTERTIUS.

UH?

BIG HEAP MENHIR MAKERS STONY BROKE!

44A

BUT ALL SUCH COMPLICATED PROBLEMS MELT AWAY UNDER THE STARS, LIKE SNOW MELTING IN THE SUN, AND THE GAULS CELEBRATE THE RE-ESTABLISHMENT OF THEIR FRIENDSHIP WITH A QUIET MIND..

44B

THE END

UDERZO & GOSCINNY